FICTION HOUSE PRESS
PRESENTS

SPICY STORIES

November 1934
Vol. 4, No. 11

This reprint edition is a facsimile of the original pulp magazine. Variations in printing and quality can be attributed to the original magazine which was printed on rough woodpulp paper.

ISBN 978-1-64720-107-4

www.FictionHousePress.com
fictionhousepress@gmail.com

NOVEMBER
1934

VOLUME 4
NUMBER 11

PEPPY STORIES

SPARKLING FEATURES

SPICY STORIES is published monthly by the D. M. Publishing Co., Inc., Wilmington, Del. William J. David, President.

Between You and Me!

Dear Editor:

I've read your magazine for quite a few years although this is the first time I have written to you. I think that the stories that your staff of writers turn out can be placed with the best of them. Since this is the first letter will you please put this into print.

I would like to have quite a few young ladies write to me on an oath that I will answer all letters written to me. I am a Frenchman by birth and like a lot of known men of that country I am small if you consider 5 feet 4 inches small. I am 20 years old, have dark brown hair and brown eyes. I will exchange photos of the near vicinity and of the fair. So write as soon as this gets into print, if it does.

Yours,

Jean Deschamps.

c/o General Delivery, Chicago, Illinois.

Dear Ed.:

Would like to hear from other readers of "Spicy"—male and female, naturally female preferred.

Am 21; 5 ft. 10 ins.; brown hair, blue eyes; rank as a leading Airman in British Air Force and anxious to get the low down on some of my American brothers and sisters who like a peppy narrative.

So let's be hearing from some of them if this letter goes into typescript.

Cheerio,

John Kemp.

24 Squadron, Royal Air Force,
Hendon, London, England.

Dear Editor:

I am a constant reader of your Spicy and enjoy it very much, also Pep, Snappy, Gay Parisienne and La Paree, and I would enjoy hearing from the girl readers of "Between You and Me," especially the young Red Heads and Blondes, and will answer all letters.

I am 26 years of age, 5 ft. 10 in.; weigh 175 lbs.; brown hair, blue eyes; so now girls get busy and do your stuff.

Charles Brown.

Box 211, Tulane, Calif.

Dear Editor:

Have read all of your excellent magazines and they can't be beaten for wonderful reading. Would like some Pen Pals, and hope you will publish this letter. Will write peppy letters myself. Am 27. Five feet 6½ inches tall. Weigh 145 pounds. Brown curly hair, grey eyes, dimples, not bad looking. Have been in the Army. Come on girls, and anyone else, write.

Success to you,

Edward "Curly" Luther.

46 Summer Street, Providence, R.I.

Dear Editor:

"Spicy" is certainly the magazine of thrills! If you want to see whether it's read from cover to cover the first day I get it every month, you ought to peek in on the radio shack of this old tin can! (Destroyer, to anybody who hasn't served a cruise in the old nyvee). We also get La Paree, Snappy, Pep, and Gay Parisienne, and all the gobs sure make a dive for them. Even the skipper swiped our last copy!

Here's my suggestion: there are certainly plenty of "hot" situations in the navy. Why not have some of your authors write a spicy story about us sailors? You've got a big audience in uniforms that would appreciate a yarn or two like that.

Yours truly,

Dave Barrett.

San Diego, Cal.

Dear Sir:

As a constant reader of Spicy Stories, I feel entitled to offer a criticism or so. Do I rate it?

I think your stories are swell—The only trouble is you take up too many pages with pictures instead of giving us more stories. Of course the photographs are good, but I think it would be a better magazine with about one or two more stories and fewer photographs. How about it?

S. M.

P. S.—When do we get more stories by Frank Kenneth Young?

(Please turn to page 62)

ONE GOOD TURN

By
GORDON SAYRE

LILY SUNDERLAND was not yet up. It was noon, but there had been a party the night before; and what a party!

Lying awake in bed, Lily thought it over in retrospect; and she had only one regret. Nice men, some of them good looking, but few of them, she suspected, with red blood.

Or was it because of her brother, she wondered. Lily and her brother lived together on Midwest Avenue, with just one servant. Lily's brother was well liked, which might, she supposed, account for the fact that she was never besieged too far by her admirers. Or maybe it was for a more serious reason. Her brother, she remembered, had been the best boxer at college; and now he was an assistant prosecuting attorney rising rapidly upon a solid foundation of personality and brains.

Whatever it was, Lily decided, that made her admirers too respectful, she was getting tired of it. She'd left home and come to the large middle western city to live with her brother, hoping it would be more exciting than middle western small town life.

She sighed, rose, and went into the bathroom, with its glistening green tiles and its magnificent sunken pool. With its mirror covered walls, and the dainty glass shelves full of scent bottles in variegated hues and bath salts in oddly shaped containters.

Unbuttoning the top part of her pyjamas she hung the sleazy bit of green silk fabric upon a hook. Dainty and rich as the fabric was it seemed like the sheerest cotton compared to what lay beneath it; for the flesh of the upper part of Lily's body was such as to shame the finest silk; and, beside, it was living, pinkly glowing well curved texture, with well fleshed shoulders that were at no point too well padded, but which were covered with not an ounce too much or an ounce too little anywhere of resilient, dimpled flesh.

Pulling a white bathing cap on over her rather unruly and naturally curly reddish gold hair she looked at herself in the glass. It took a very pretty face to stand such a test.

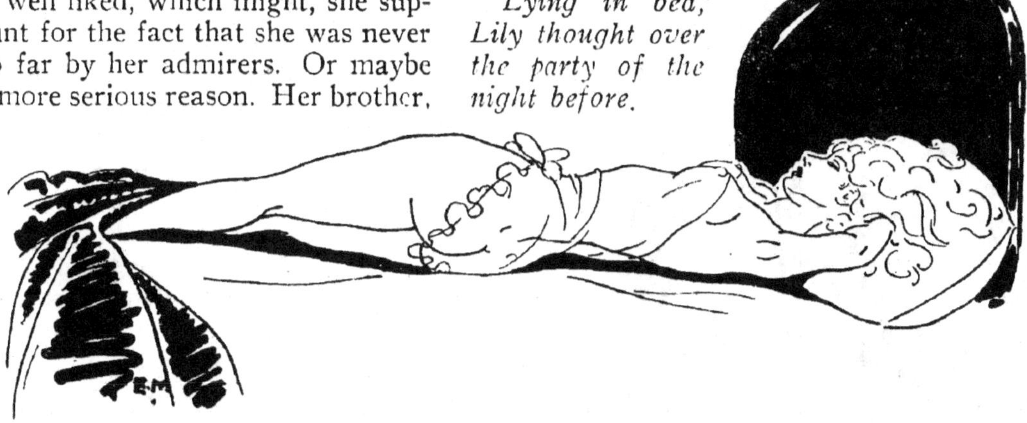

Lying in bed, Lily thought over the party of the night before.

But Lily's face would still have been pretty, even if you subtracted her slim throat as well and set the head all by itself upon a table. Large, darkly blue eyes that seemed almost violet in some lights. A prettily rounded and dimpled, but nevertheless firm chin. Cheeks naturally pink and dimpled, and rounded out to just the proper point to make the almost perfect oval of her face. A tiny, retrousse, provocative nose, with delicate nostrils that twitched when she was excited; which was often, since Lily was only tweny, and very much in love with life and her own glowing, vital youth.

Lips that were small, and that sometimes, when she didn't get what she wanted in a hurry, pouted a bit fetchingly. Lips not thick nor yet thin; lips that were perfect and made especially for kisses. Hot lips, always just freshly damp, and, even without touching up, healthily red.

Stepping upon the scales built into the floor she noted that her five feet five inches still carried just neatly the hundred and twenty pounds that rounded out every one of her soft curves but still made her seem slim as a dancing, woodland elf.

Looking into the mirror opposite the scales she tested the consistency of her breasts, as against the possibility of their ever getting to droop, which seemed extremely unlikely, since they pouted out almost pointed from a snowy expanse of bosom; their tips, in the warm bathroom, pinkly tempting and unwrinkled, like little rose buds.

Convinced that all was still well with her, Lily stepped into the bath and turned on the shower. After a brisk cool shower she allowed warm water to collect in the tub, filled it with the loveliest of bath salts and sat down in it, lying back, on the sloping edge of the tub, and stretching out while her body was impregnated with a scent so soft and so sensual that it seemed, rather than an artificial perfume, a soft accentuation of her own sweet bodily odors.

Getting up she let the water out and rubbed down swiftly with a moss thick and soft Turkish towel, which brought a deeply pink tinge to her body, making it seem something almost ethereally beautiful. It was then that she heard voices out in the hall. She had left the bathroom door open a bit so as not to exhaust the air in the room.

She heard the frightened exclamation of her maid, and then a gruff voice saying:

"All you got to do is keep your trap shut, sister, and nothing will happen to you; let a yap out of you or make a false move and you'll get blasted. Keep your eye on her every minute, Nick, and if she so much as makes a face at you, let her have it."

Lily started to dash for the door, intending to lock it; but, just as she started for it she heard a man come down the hall. She fled back to the security of the shower curtain and hid there trembling. Finally she heard the bathroom door swing open. And then, after a minute, she heard a chuckle from the intruder.

Immediately she guessed its cause. Her tiny feet with their jewel-like nails, and her slim ankles, and at least half of a shapely calf showed beneath the shower curtain.

"Come out of there," a contralto rather nice male voice demanded. Lily peeked through the curtain and saw a young man of not over twenty-five. He was flawlessly dressed in a dark brown suit which perfectly fitted him and exactly matched huge, dark brown eyes. His hair was jet black, and so carefully molded to a well set head that not a single hair seemed to be out of place.

He was handsome, in a foreign sort of way; she guessed that he might well be from the

Argentine. His features were sharply cut and almost fawn like in their accentuation. He had wide shoulders and slim hips, and stood very erect and squarely. His brown eyes laughed.

SHE LOOKED DOWN at the small but uncompromising black gun in his hand. She resorted to pleading:

"Aw, please go away."

"It's all right, sister; you don't need to worry. I'm not going to hurt you. Just intend to throw a scare into that brother of yours and give him an idea what *might* happen if he raids one of Tony Lazarri's places again."

"I'll bet they're nasty places, or he wouldn't raid them. He's a good sport."

"They're not nasty places; they're gambling joints, and they're on the level, and he knows it."

She heard him move across the floor. Suddenly there was the hiss of water turned on. Hot water!—and her feet were right in the pool. She tried to yank the curtain from its fastenings; but it wouldn't come. She reached out from the curtain, grabbed a towel off the rack, wrapped it around her middle before the hot water reached her feet, and then sprang out of the tub.

"Oh! Lady!" he gasped in appreciation. "Listen: I've taken some neat tricks in my time; but, honest to goodness, lady, I *never* seen anything to compare."

"You let me out of here to go and get some clothes on or I—"

"My brother will make mince meat of you for this."

"Aw, who's afraid of the big bad wolf?"

"Go away, please!"

He remained and stared, much impressed.

"That's quite enough of this," she remarked primly; but it was hard to be prim, and it was hard to be forceful with burning brown eyes heating up her breasts with avid glances.

"You let me out of here to go and get some clothes on or I—" she thought over assorted threats in her mind; there didn't seem to be much of anything that would frighten this laughing-eyed satyr with a deadly weapon in his rather fine looking hand. ". . . Or I won't like you at all!"

"Ho! Ho!" he laughed, imitating a pirate.

But he stood uncompromisingly blocking the way to the door.

"What are you going to do?" she asked feebly.

"What do you think?" he asked, and his eyes, which had been smoldering all along seemed to flame.

"I—don't want to think, if you don't mind," Lily temporized.

"Well, lookit, baby; suppose you be nice to me and maybe I won't be so rough as I was going to be. You know, I planned on scaring you out of ten years' growth when I came in here; and I really ought to at that—it would be nice if you could stay looking just as you are now for another ten years—but, honest, I kind of like you, just as I really like your brother . . . both of us, him and me, are in a racket—there's no reason why we shouldn't get along together; and we will when he gets over some of those wild ideas every young prosecutor has at first."

"That's all very well; but will you stop staring at me that way and let me go get some clothes on!"

"Take it easy, baby; jeez, can't a guy even look at you?"

"Sure, but, the way you're looking, it's practically the same as — I don't know what . . . !"

"Tell you what you do," he temporized; "give me a little kiss and I'll run along."

"No!" She stamped her feet and the towel slipped a full inch.

"Oooooop!" he warned, "be careful!"

She yanked the towel up.

"Going to give me that kiss, baby, or shall I take it?"

"Just one?" she bargained.

"One will be enough; but let me end it."

"All right," she agreed.

He stepped close to her. Lily felt vibrations that were not of short wave length intensity.

It was a kiss such as the kind Lily had often dreamed of experiencing but had never before known in real life. It lasted so long that Lily almost completely ran out of air; but she didn't care whether she could breathe or not.

She was frightened; desperately so—but, like the three little pigs she rather enjoyed being frightened that way.

Her arms went up and around his neck, without her having consciously willed or directed them to do so.

Suddenly she was brought back to present consciousness by realization of the fact that the towel was again slipping. She sprang away from him and retrieved it. But she didn't need to be afraid of him. Like a man in a daze he walked backward until the back of his knees struck a stool with a glass top. He sat down weakly for a minute; finally looked up at her:

"Say!" he asked. "What did you hit me with?"

"I 'hit you'? What are you talking about?"

"Oh . . . ! Baby!" he sighed and started to get up. This time she was really frightened.

"You stay where you are," she warned, "or I will hit you with something."

"But what's the dope, baby? You seem to like being kissed by me as much as I like kissing you? What's the stall?" He continued to advance. Frantically she bargained:

"Look," she pled, "let me alone and I'll promise you something."

"Yeh?" he stopped, and now some of the kindliness and humor came back to his handsome eyes; but he looked as though he only reluctantly withheld himself from the sweetest tidbit that very wise eyes had ever seen.

"If you'll go away now and let me alone I'll promise that my brother won't raid you any more, and that you needn't worry about getting into trouble for breaking in here either.

"But suppose your brother won't consent not to—to stop—"

"All right, I'll go farther than that," she frantically promised.

"If he ever raids you again I give you my word of honor that I'll come to you at any place you name."

"Is that on the level, baby?"

"Yes."

"Well, my main place is at Hogarth and Hawthorne Streets; you go into the restaurant and ask for Tony; the lookout looks you over and calls me; if you're O. K. and there's nobody with you he takes you to me through a passage the dicks can't find. But you better not double-cross me—I'm telling you something."

"I won't—honest I won't—only go. And if he raids you again I give you my word I'll keep my promise."

"Do you really want me to go?" he mourned.

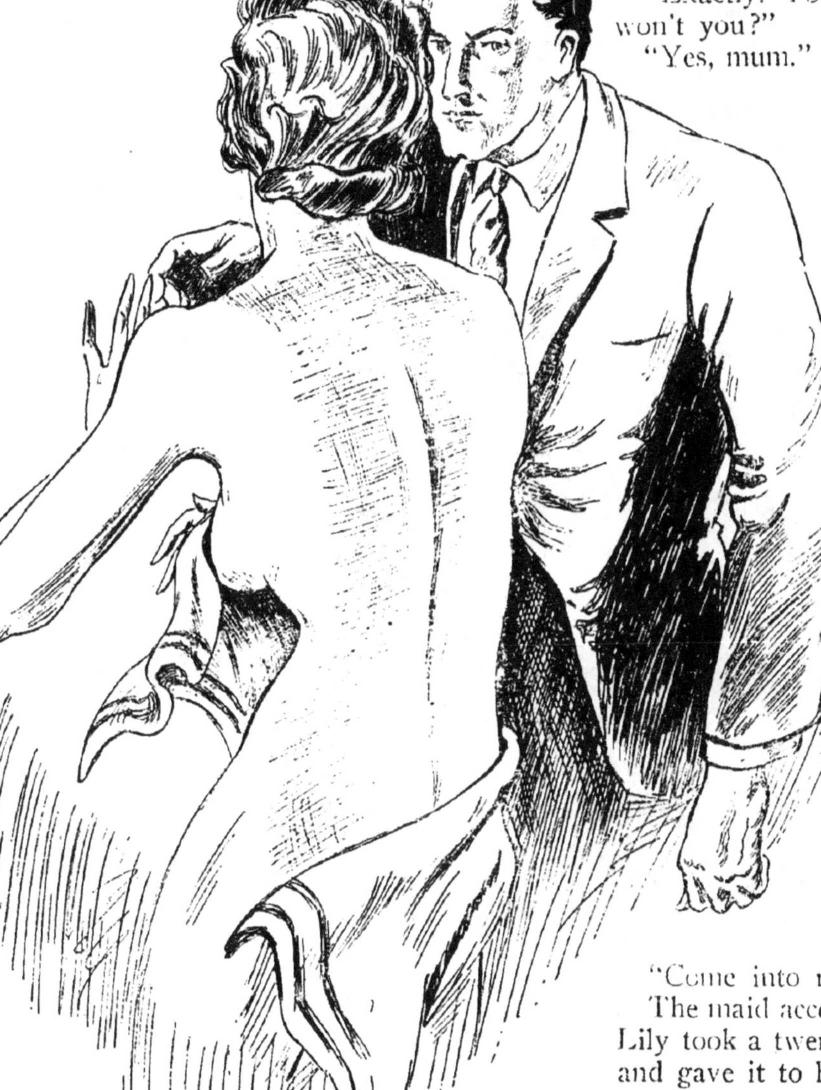

". . . Going to give me that kiss, baby, or shall I take it?"

"Yes—and you promised, you know—after one kiss."

"All right," he agreed; and with one last look at her lovely breasts which she had forgotten to cover with her rather inadequate small hands he went down the hall, called to his bodyguard, and the front door banged behind them.

Suffering from nervous reaction Lily flew down the hall and grabbed the phone out of the maid's hands.

"Don't do that," she warned, "and you must not, under any circumstances, tell my brother, or anyone, about this. Do you understand?"

"Yes, Mam, I unerstand; you don't want it to get into the papers and you're afraid your brother might get hurt if he heard about it and tried to kill that lug."

"Exactly. You will keep quiet, then, Mary, won't you?"

"Yes, mum."

"Come into my room," Lily directed.

The maid accompanied her to the bedroom. Lily took a twenty-dollar bill from her purse and gave it to her.

"Now go away and leave me alone," Lily directed.

When the maid had gone and shut the door, Lily lay down upon her perfumed, silk covered bed and threw away the towel. She stretched out and dreamily closed her eyes. For a long time she lay thus; and then she took up the phone: called her brother.

"Hello, sweetheart," he greeted cheerfully.

"Listen, Walt, you ever hear of a gangster named 'Tony Lazarri'?"

(*Please turn to page* 61)

WICKED

The concluding instalment of a two-part story

By
ARTHUR WALLACE

"Don't you trust that Burt Cooksley with anything, Mister," she told him.

(Synopsis of Part One—Vince Garner, author of smart, "society" novels, goes West at the suggestion of his publisher to write a real study of real people. Alice Van Pell, daughter of the socially prominent Van Pells, and Vince's fiancee, objects, but nevertheless he goes. It is understood they will marry on his return. At a "square" dance in the mountain country he has chosen as his locale, Vince meets Dale Silsby, characterized by Burt Cooksley, a truck farmer, as "a wicked girl". Dale intrigues Vince and he engages her to come to his mountain cottage and cook and clean for him. The very first night he is tormented with her full-blown, natural beauty. She is sleeping on a mattress stretched on the floor; he on a couch. Vince finally dozes off, comparing Dale to his fiancee, Alice.)

PART TWO

THE SUN was streaming in through the east windows when Vince stirred under the coverlets, opened his eyes and stretched his arms above his head. The pungent, satisfying odor of coffee reached his nostrils. He could hear the sputter of something frying. He swung his feet off the couch and reached for his pants. Two minutes later he was dousing his head under the hand pump in the yard.

When Vince came back to the house, he ran a comb through his wet hair and sauntered into the kitchen. Dale was frying strips of bacon on a skillet. Yellow hominy bubbled in a pot. Coffee simmered in another. A heap of brown biscuits kept warm on the stove ledge.

"Gee, this smells good," Vince commented. "You must have gotten up early, Dale."

She nodded without turning her head. "Always do. Only city folks hanker to stay abed. T'ain't good."

Vince rubbed his shaven chin and smiled ruefully. Morning cheerfulness seemed to be lost on the alleged hoyden of Potter's Place, Nevada. He seated himself at the tiny table as she ladled out a generous portion of cereal. Between spoonfulls he studied her in the revealing light of day. Her hair was a tawny brown mane, drawn back from her face and bunched in a knot at the nape of her neck. Vince was amazed at the perfection of her complexion, but even more so, the regularity of her features. A straight, aquiline nose, the nostrils firm and sensitive, was spaced beautifully between large, expressive eyes and red lips that were red without benefit of lipstick.

Above all, her body fascinated Vince with its firm, full-breasted strength. He was reminded of a Rivera mural he had seen in Mexico City; a vital, living thing depicting the liberation of the female sex.

There had been nothing fragile or delicate about the painting, just as there was nothing fragile and delicate about Dale Silsby. The men were tall, rangy, hard-boned spawns of the earth, and the women, full-breasted, wide-hipped and radiating lusty physical well-being.

Dale could have posed for the Rivera mural. She yielded nothing to the maduro-tinted women of the South. Her shoulders were broad and erect, almost masculine in their depth. From armpits, damp with the heat of the coal stove, her tanned flesh curved out to form the superbly resilient outlines of round breasts. As Vince watched her bosom rise and fall beneath a thin cotton dress, he realized what it must mean to be an artist, to create living images with brush or scalpel. He could paint the picture of those breasts in words, but only on canvas or in marble could justice be done to their compelling firmness.

And even then, he thought, paint was flat and without substance and sculpture cold and lifeless. His eyes traveled down the undulating line of her figure, visually caressing her flat waist, maternal hips and strong, columnar thighs.

She turned and pushed a plate of bacon and eggs in front of him. The appetite-quickening odor of them eddied up and teased his nostrils. A steaming cup of coffee and the hot biscuits were at his side.

"This is swell!" he said. looking up at her.

She averted her eyes and sniffed audibly. "Nothin' special. Couldn't find no real flour or I'd make flapjacks." She picked a red box from the stove. "This here prepared flour ain't much good, 'cept fer biscuits an' even then it ain't so good. You need some flour an' some bakin' soda an' some potatoes. I don't see how you been eatin' up here."

Vince laughed. "I'll get Burt Cooksley to bring everything up when he fetches the bed for you."

She turned angrily, her eyes flashing. It was the first display of feeling Vince had seen her show and he stopped eating to admire it.

"Don't you trust that Burt Cooksley with anythin', Mister. He'll cheat you out of your eye teeth. I seen the load of turnips he sold you. Most of 'em is wormy."

The girl was superb in emotion. Her eyes spit fire and her bosom filled out magnificently. "All right, Dale, I'll get someone else," he said. "I'll take the morning off and drive into town. Do you want to come along?"

She shook her head. "No. If my Pap sees me he'll beat hell out of me. Just drop by an' give him my first week's pay. That'll keep him drunk fer a while."

Vince rode into Potter's Place and drew up before the Post Office. Inside he met Cooksley. The farmer was carrying a huge mail order catalogue.

"How do, Mister Garner?" he greeted.

Vince smiled cheerily. "Hello, Mr. Cooksley." He approached the window and nodded pleasantly to the elderly postmaster. "Anything today?"

Two letters, one typewritten, the other in a familiar hand came through the window.

"Rain much on the mountain, Mister Garner?" the postmaster queried, peering over his specs.

"A little, but I don't mind. By the way, where can I locate Franklin Silsby?"

"Frank Silsby? He's over yonder by the feed mill. You know where Turner's farm is, don't you? The big white barn on the road? Well, you go a pace past the barn an' there's a road goin' right. T'ain't much of a road, just a cow path, but at the end of it you'll find Frank Silsby's place providin' he's there."

Vince smiled at the rural exactness of direction sparkling with human sidelights. "Thanks," he said.

Cooksley confronted him at the door. "Everythin' all right, Mister Garner?" he questioned inquisitively, his lean jaws working away furiously.

"Perfectly fine, Mr. Cooksley."

The road leading to Frank Silsby's nondescript farm was no road to speak of, as the postmaster had pointed out. Vince jounced up and down in the seat as the Ford navigated foot-deep ruts and jagged holes. Finally a ramshackle house came into view and he guided the car into the yard. Minutes of tooting the horn drew a dirty, hairy individual from behind once white chicken coops. He approached slowly, pushing a worn felt hat back on his head and mopping a wet brow with a filthy handkerchief.

"How do," he greeted, one foot perched on the running board.

Vince returned the salutation. "You're Franklin Silsby, aren't you?" he queried.

The individual nodded. "Yup, that's me, stranger."

"Well, I'm Vince Garner. I rented a cottage in the mountains and your daughter, Dale, is working for me."

Silsby spat viciously. "Pleased to meet cha, Mister Garner, but that wench should oughtta be whipped. T'ain't the fust time she ain't showed up fer a night an' by cracky I tole her—"

Vince brought a five dollar bill out of his pocket. "She said to give you her first week's pay," he began.

The farmer's eyes brightened. He reached for the greenback and fondled it like a child fondles a new penny.

"Always wuz thinkin' of her Pap," he beamed. "Dale's a good gal even if she is a mite wild. Not havin' a woman around's been the ruinin' of her." He stretched the bill out. "You agoin' to pay her this much every week, Mister?" he asked dubiously.

"Yes, Mr. Silsby. Every week." He stepped on the gas, indicating the interview was over. The farmer doffed his hat.

"Much obliged fer comin' over, Mister Garner. I'll be seein' ya."

In town again, Vince purchased a second hand bed from the hotel, loaded it into the back of the Ford, purchased a week's supply of groceries and canned goods and was about to start again and walked inside.

"Have you any girl's dresses?" he inquired of a pimply-faced youth who perambulated his gawky frame from behind a counter.

"Whut size gal?"

Vince gulped. "Oh, I really couldn't say. I guess she's about five feet five inches tall."

"Whut heft?"

"You've got me now. Do you know Dale Silsby?"

The boy blushed. "Who don't, Mister?"

"Well, the dresses should fit her."

Ten minutes after Vince had guided the car up the mountain, the news that he had purchased three dimity dresses for Dale Silsby had gone the rounds of Potter's Place. It was news the like of which had not been circulated since Hutch Connor's wife had run off with a medicine man from Iowa.

Vince lifted the bed frame from the car as Dale unloaded the groceries. When she came to the package, squeezed it speculatively and then shot quizzical eyes in his direction.

"It's just a couple of dresses. I thought maybe—"

Before he could finish the sentence she was in the house, tearing the brown paper off the package. Vince smiled and busied himself unloading the bed spring. He was just about to step into the car again to drive it under the shed when Dale came out of the cabin, cheeks flushed and eyes glittering like diamond chips. She was wearing one of the dresses: the pink one. It seemed to fit perfectly and rather than conceal her lush charms, brought them out vividly. Her breasts seemed smaller and more compact under a semi-tight bodice. The excuse for style gave her lower torso a certain grace and carriage.

She rushed up to Vince, wisps of hair flying in the breeze. Her brown arms shot about his neck and the next moment he felt the blinding, blood-tingling pressure of her damp, parted lips on his mouth. Unconsciously his own arms circled her waist. He could feel the warmth of her figure against his palms.

She drew her lips away with slow, excruciating torture, but her body still clung, flint-tipped breasts boring into his chest.

Vince tried to catch his breath, succeeding as she stepped away.

"Thanks a lot, Mister Garner," she whispered. "I ain't had a new dress for a long time."

Once more she was just a simple, basic country girl endowed with an aura of wickedness. In his arms, the tantalizing rapture of her full mouth and the sweet pressure of her body had transformed her into an exotic mountain siren. Vince was afraid for the future. He had tasted heady wine and the intoxication of it bubbled in his blood.

Long after he had put the car up and set the bed in a corner of the room, Vince remembered he was carrying two letters in his back pocket; one from Tilton, his publisher, and the other from Alice, his fiancee. He read the publisher's letter first. It was a request—an urgent request—for the first few chapters of the novel.

> ". . . *I'd like to get a line on it, Vince, for some advance publicity* . . ." Sam Tilton wrote. "*The critics are all kidding the idea of your doing a realistic book and* . . ."

Alice's letter was more demonstrative, more demanding. Vince smiled as he read it.

> ". . . *I'm the laughing stock of my friends and only because of your silly idea. If you don't return immediately and live like a normal man, I'll come up and get you! Mother says* . . ."

Vince put the letter aside. He always put Alice's communications aside when she arrived at he point: "Mother says . . .".

Filling his pipe and lighting it, he sat down at his typewriter, slipped a sheet of paper into the roller and typed, in capital letters, in the middle of the sheet, the word: *WICKED*. Beneath it, in upper and lower case: *by Vince Garner*.

For three hours, until Dale announced lunch, he worked furiously. The words seemed to flow from his finger-tips and form rich, well-rounded sentences without any effort on his part. Somehow, his entire aspect of the theme had changed. He was writing about something so close to him now that it was almost dangerous. The essence of the story lived and breathed in the next room. He leaned back in his chair and read over the last paragraph. It seemed to swing along like a rhythmic mountain song and he liked it.

Her brown arms shot up around his neck. . . .

"She was young, but her body was ripe with the ripeness of the earth, the velvet smoothness of the purple plum, the maturity of things that grow and are warm in the soft loam that gives them birth. The mechanical genius of man, the fabulous reality of buildings and bridges and steel spans stretching for miles, were as nothing to the physical profundity of her breasts. Each tiny cell of her seemed to call out and say: 'I am life! I come from life! Nothing transcends me! My breasts, my hips, my body breathe with the breath of life! I am real!'."

Vince rose from his chair. Nineteen pages in three hours was pretty good work. He felt

"Folks is always sayin' I ain't no good," she said in a low voice.

satisfied. By the end of the week he would have fifeen thousand words for Tilton. Let the critics laugh! This novel, unlike his others, would be real if nothing else!

A wagon drew up before the door. Vince recognized Burt Cooksley's weather-beaten face. He walked out into the yard.

"Don't need any turnips, Mr. Cooksley," he said, "but you can do something for me. I have to send a telegram and I want you to give it to the operator in town to send for me. I'll write it out for you."

Vince walked inside and scribbled Alice Van Pell's address on a piece of paper. Beneath it he wrote the message:

"Don't be a child.—Vince."

He was in the yard again before the curious Cooksley could come off the wagon seat. "Here, Mr. Cooksley, take this down at once," he said, forestalling any movement. "Here's a dollar for the telegram and a dollar for you. Hurry it up!"

The afternoon went by quickly. Vince, working at breakneck speed without feeling any strain, called a halt as the sun started to dip beneath the hills. All told he had forty-three pages, almost ten thousand words, completed. He was satisfied, too, that it needed little revision.

Dale was strangely silent during the evening meal. She seemed to be mulling something over in her mind. At intervals, she would steal glances at Vince, but when his eyes met hers, she turned away.

Later, when it was dark and they were sitting in the large room, she spoke, her fingers toying with the pleats of her new dress.

"Didn't nobody say nasty things about me in town?" she asked.

Vince lowered the magazine he was reading. "Why, no, Dale. What makes you ask that?"

Her eyes followed the movement of her hands. "Nuthin'. I just thought they did. Folks is always sayin' I ain't no good."

"Why do they say that, Dale?"

She shrugged. "Dunno. Guess it's 'cause I like to be happy and have a lot of fun. Guess it's 'cause I don't sit to home an' do the chores."

Suddenly, like a hunted, frightened thing, she left her chair and crouched at Vince's feet. She was sobbing softly as he lifted her up and eased her into his lap. Her body against him was warm and soft. By accident the back of his hand brushed a round breast and he could feel the tremor of it go through him. He bent his head and kissed her brow, but somehow the paternal gesture seemed weak and anaemic. The very passion of her contact was contagious.

Vince fought the lure but it was too much for him. His hands, traveling over her, found the solace his soul cried out for. Beneath his fingers her breasts seemed to swell and quiver. She breathed softly, lifting her face. Vince's lips met the warmth of her mouth, drank the heady nectar of it. He shivered. Flashes of Alice, cold and aloof passed through his mind. Cocktail parties . . . dinner engagements . . . night clubs. . . . What did they mean compared to this?

He rose, lifting her up with him. She was like a feather in his arms. He stumbled to the couch, dropped down beside her. Eager fingers fumbled with her bodice, reached for round softness. It was sweet. . . .

"MISTER GARNER!"

Vince froze. It was Burt Cooksley's voice booming from outside the door. He rose slowly, and walked to the door.

"Yes?"

"Mister Garner!"

Vince opened the door bare inches. Cooksley's jaw shot into the aperture. "Got someone to see yer, Mister Garner."

A figure stepped up behind him and pushed the door open, taking Vince by surprise. He stared, amazed, as Alice Van Pell's steel-gray eyes bored through him. Her very silence was cutting, like the honed edge of a razor. Suddenly, from the couch, came a sigh. Alice's head turned. She looked at Dale, recumbent, the upper halves of her white breasts shimmering with alabaster brilliance. Cooksley, directly behind her, wet his thin, tobacco-stained lips.

"So they were right?" Alice cried. "They were right when they told me you were buying dresses for a—for a—" The foul word formed on her lips.

"Shut up!" Vince's facial muscles tensed.

She snickered. "So, that's the attraction, is it? I should have thought as much. A *real* story of *real* people? Hmmph! You mean a real affair with a real—!"

Vince pointed to the door. "You can get out and stay out! Take your dirty tinsel of refinement with you! You're nothing but a cheap imitation of a woman! You call other people names!" He pointed to Dale, now sitting up, crying softly. "There's more realness in her little toe than in your whole body! Now, get!"

When the door had closed, Vince walked to the couch. His heart was full with the victory over himself. He felt clean and purged. The very orchidaceous odor of Alice, her painted finger-nails and artificially colored lips had gone against his grain. Now he wondered how he had ever accepted the sham of her.

Down on his knees he kissed away Dale's frightened tears.

"Don't cry, Dale," he whispered. "If anything I do from now on is worth while, it will be because of you. Nothing I have ever done has mattered much and it was because of her."

His lips nestled in the warm, pulsating hollow of her throat. "Don't mind what they say, Dale. Let the whole world call you wicked." They melted into each other's arms. "I—I know you're real."

RAIN

THE moon shed tear-drops every time we kissed.
The wind moaned through the leaves each time I said
That we would never part. The rain-drops hissed
About us when I gently stroked your head.

AND so we said the dripping clouds were jealous
And roaring out their anguish from above
But now, we have experience to tell us
They hated us for being fools in love.

—*By Sid.*

TANGLED WIVES!

By

DIANA PAGE

PART ONE

THE SODA syphon in the practiced hands of Don Harwood hissed very pleasantly as he squirted an exact proportion of its bubbling contents into two tall, ice-filled glasses already liberally spiked by a jigger of scotch.

To Paul Creston, idly resting an elbow on the dining room buffet, he handed one glass and kept the other for himself.

"Good hunting, mine host!" exclaimed Paul. "That's what they used to say over a tankard of creamy ale in the old days."

"Drink hearty!" Don rejoined.

Glancing at the strap watch below the gleaming white cuff of his evening shirt, Paul remarked:

"If those girls aren't ready soon, we'll be getting to that dance in time to turn around and go home."

"Give them plenty of time, old boy!" said Don, tinkling the ice in his glass. "Women shouldn't be rushed, you know."

Paul smiled. "So they tell me!"

Snatches of feminine laughter and chatter drifted out to them from an adjacent bedroom.

"They seem to be having a good time, anyway!" remarked Don, seating himself.

"They should be pepped up!" Paul drawled. "Those cocktails Sylvia mixed before dinner were powerful medicine."

"Uh-huh!" commented Don. "My wife has the reputation of shaking a wicked shaker."

"So's mine!" declared Paul, laughing. "Mabel seems to think that a cocktail should be seven-eights gin and one-eighth vermouth . . . she says the ice weakens the gin, shortening its kick, so the recipe for a good martini is all wrong."

Don chuckled. "Sylvia likes to experiment with an old-fashioned, and most of her scientific research is bent upon finding out how much rye the glass will hold after the fruit is in."

"Good pals, those gals of ours!" said Paul. "By the way, weren't we talking about a week-end in the mountains before the snow flies?"

"Oh, yes!" Don exclaimed.

"Listen!" Paul took a deep swig of his highball. "We could leave on Friday afternoon . . . "

IN THE BEDROOM, Sylvia Harwood was concentrating upon the artistic job of accentuating the pretty bow of her lips with the aid of a scarlet lipstick. Shaded boudoir lamps, on the dressing table at which she was sitting, pinked the paleness of her skin so daringly bared by the design of her evening gown, and stressed the silvery tints of light blonde hair brushed straight back from a high forehead and arranged in a silky coil on the nape of her neck.

"Do you think I ought to wear a slip or a brassiere or something under this dress?" She looked at herself in the mirror, studying the lines of the garment, which was the costume of a sophisticate. Its decolletage extended in back to the spinal dip at her waist, and in the front two cup-shaped strips of transparent velvet, held in place by a pair of rhinestone shoulder straps, moulded the lush fullness of twin breasts.

Mabel Creston lowered the tiny brush with which she was painting her eyelashes in a shade of mascara that matched the chestnut hue of her hair.

"Well, darling, it does look like a coming-out party!" she replied, smiling.

"Am I showing too much?" asked Sylvia.

"You'd almost be in costume for a masquerade ball as a member of a nudist's colony!" said Mabel.

"As bad as that?" Sylvia arched an eyebrow.

"As good, you mean!" laughed Mabel.

"Then I guess I've got to strap myself in with a brassiere." Sylvia stamped her foot petulantly. "And how I hate the darn things! They bind me suffocatingly, and I never bought one in my life that didn't spoil the lines of a gown in front."

She delved into a bureau drawer, but Mabel stopped her.

"Don't be silly!" the latter said. "I was only kidding. You look stunning exactly as you are. Don't forget you have a figure that's worth showing. . . . I'm envious."

Mabel glanced at the pertly rounded little breasts that sprang from her own bosom. "These cuties of mine never did grow up!" she added.

Sylvia fussed the transparent velvet cups, spreading them so that they covered as large an area as possible. "Then you think I can take a chance like this?"

"Ready? The boys will be thinking we're lost."

"Yes!" replied Mabel, tossing a wrap on her shoulders. "It's getting late, too!"

Sylvia paused for effect in the dining room doorway, exclaiming:

"Oh, look at the lonesome drinkers! We can't allow that, can we, Mabel?"

"Indeed not!" Mabel shook a reproving finger. "Where's mine?"

"Do you think I ought to wear a slip or something under this dress?" Sylvia questioned.

"You might create a sensation at the dance, but I guess the gown will be all right if you don't stoop." Mabel's eyes sparkled teasingly. "And you'd better watch that husband of mine. Paul is very partial to such soft beauties, especially when he has had a few drinks."

Sylvia turned back to her dressing table. She might have admitted that she had already found out Paul's liking for voluptuous fondling and flirtatious play. She drew a perfumed wand across her lips, picked up her cloak and said:

"And mine!" added Sylvia.

Don strolled to the buffet and spiked two fresh glasses.

"It's your fault!" declared Paul. "You left us stranded here, and what is there for two forsaken men to do but try to drown their sorrows in drink?"

"We were making ourselves pretty for you!" said Sylvia, fluttering her lashes at him.

"And you certainly succeeded!" he mur-

(Please turn to page 54)

FIFTY DOLLARS

By
E. J. CRESCENT

TERRY McCALL would not be budged —either from his seat by the fire or from the subject in hand. He stuck doggedly to both, and the more Ilsa paced and fumed, the more determined he seemed to be that she should come to a show-down. Snow fluttered against the window pane, the fire burned brightly, and he was perfectly content to sit there the rest of the night. Ilsa, a Japanese kimono flung over a set of sky-blue silk underwear, fluttered about the room, running her fingers through her red hair and looking distrait. Finally, she turned to him, and with considerable vehemence, said,

"Terry, will you please go and leave me alone?"

"No," answered Terry, and there seemed to be little doubt but what he meant it.

"But what in the world can you want with me?" demanded Ilsa.

"I want to know the reason for the sudden blast of ice," said Terry.

"There isn't any reason. I just don't love you anymore. Can't you understand? I just don't love you any more!"

Terry crossed his legs and stared unseeingly into the fire. "If you were a different type of girl, Ilsa," he said, "I'd believe you without question, and that would be that. As it is, I don't believe you. It isn't conceit. You don't behave as though you don't love me any more. If you didn't love me any more, you wouldn't be so upset because I won't go." He turned and grinned at her. "Why don't you get it off your chest, and tell me the whole sad story?"

"There's nothing to get off my chest," snapped Ilsa, "and there isn't any sad story."

"Ah, but there must be. Have I done something you don't like?"

For a moment Ilsa didn't answer. Instead she took a brief turn or two about the room, ending up with her back to the fire, facing Terry. He could see right through her, and that didn't help at all. After a while, she said,

"Terry, have you ever stopped to consider what a couple of rats we are—you and I?"

Terry grinned again. "Can't say that I ever have," he admitted.

"Well, we are. Just a couple of rats. And I'm tired of it. God knows, I thought it bad enough being a show girl, but this racket . . ." She shook her head sadly.

"What's the matter with this racket?" demanded Terry. "It pays well, and it isn't too dishonest."

"Neither is it too decent."

"I don't see that at all. If the laws of this state are so archaic that a couple of people can't get a divorce without going to a lot of expense and trouble, why are we rats for making it easier for them?"

"It isn't that. It's the way we have to go about it. My God, how many times have I been the Unknown Woman for fifty dollars?"

"I don't know. Hundreds I should think. I know you've made a lot of money."

"And lost a lot of self-respect." Terry eyed her keenly.

"Who's been talking to you?" he asked.

"Don't be a fool, Terry. I just don't think it's right. I've always wanted to live the right life, and everything seems to've conspired against me. First I was a showgirl, then a model, now this. How d'you think I'm going to end up? Don't you think I can see the writing on the wall, Terry?"

"You may be able to see it; but you're not reading it correctly. It says: 'Marry Terry McCall'."

Ilsa laughed nastily. "A cheap divorce detective who makes a living providing evidence that never existed. A perjurer, that's what you are, Terry—a perjurer!"

"I'm crazy about you."

"I was crazy about you once. But that's over now. I'm through with all this sort of thing. I'm going to lead the kind of life I've always wanted to lead."

Terry subjected her to a searching look. Presently he said, "What's his name, Ilsa?"

"I won't tell you."

"Ah! Then there is someone. I knew there was. What is he? A reformer or something like that?"

FOR A MOMENT it seemed that Ilsa was going to close up, then the dam burst and she threw herself onto the couch beside Terry.

Rapturously, she said, "He's a wonderful person, Terry, and he thinks I'm a wonderful person. He doesn't smoke, he doesn't drink, he's thirty-five and he's not only never been married, but he's never been in love. I'm the first woman in his life."

"That should be interesting for you," remarked Terry dryly.

"It is. It's refreshing. It's so different. He's so shy, so tender, and there are so many things I'll be able to show him." Terry laughed. "I don't mean what you mean, you louse," snapped Ilsa.

"Does he know anything about you?"

"He only knows what I've chosen to tell him . . . and that hasn't been much. He wouldn't understand, and I don't want to spoil anything."

"I quite understand. Has he been up here?"

"Yes . . . please don't do that, Terry . . ."

"How did you explain the joint? It's quite nice, and it obviously cost money."

"Terry . . . please! I told him I had a private income. He believed me. Terry, if you don't stop I'll have to move." She did move in fact. Closer to Terry. His hand was on her naked upper arm, stroking it gently, and although Ilsa knew that she should break away while there was yet time, she did not have the strength of will to do so. After all—Terry.

"How long have you known this guy?"

"He isn't a guy, and I've known him about a month."

"You're crazy. Are you going to marry him?"

"Yes. Terry, you'll tear it! Please. If you must do that, slip the shoulder strap off . . . " Ilsa looked down at his hand. It seemed quite natural to have Terry's hand on her breast, and she moved a little closer.

"When're you going to marry the guy?"

"In about a month. He's gone to Chicago to settle some business affairs. When he gets back, we're going to get married. In the meantime, get me all the jobs you can so that I can get the finest trousseau you've ever seen."

"I don't want to see it. I like what you've got on. Why not take it off?"

"Oh, Terry! Now, look here, if I do, and if I allow you to make love to me, you mustn't get the impression that it means anything. It doesn't. I'm only doing it because it's snowing, you won't go home and there doesn't seem to be anything else to do."

"Three swell reasons."

Ilsa got to her feet and slipped out of the Japanese kimono. Pensively, she said, "I wish I could show you a picture of him, Terry. But you might meet him and say something that'ud spoil everything."

"I'm not likely to meet him," answered Terry, watching the play of the firelight on Ilsa's long, white legs.

Ilsa dropped the kimono to the back of a chair. She stood with her back to the fire warming herself. Terry gazed at her lovely figure. Ilsa said, "He's so good looking, Terry. Tall, dark and sad, kind of. After we're married, I'll have you out to the house for supper some time."

"Thanks. Where're you going to live?"

"Either Jackson Heights or Flatbush. We haven't decided yet."

"Ilsa!"

"Yes? Oh, pardon me . . . " She rejoined him on the couch and looked up at him. "All the same, Terry," she said, "this is fun, isn't it?"

"Yes. It's going to feel strange having the same kind of fun with another man."

"Yes, I suppose it is. But I guess I'll get used to it, Terry. I must say, though, I like our kind of fun, don't you?"

"Uh-huh."

"Kiss me, Terry. This sort of thing doesn't seem right unless the man kisses the girl."

So Terry kissed her, and her arms stole about his neck. The firelight flickered on her white thighs and her coral-crested bosom. She stayed in Terry's arms as quietly and as contentedly as a kitten, and as his hands slid gently over her, he wondered how he could possibly break up this stupid scheme of hers. He knew that talking to her was useless. She simply couldn't see reason. Ilsa had always been governed by the emotion of the moment, and this new man had somehow managed to open up a side of her which Terry had never realized existed.

It was not very long before Ilsa commenced to respond to Terry's love-making. She stirred in his arms, and her lips continually sought his. Her sharp fingernails traced a scorching pattern along the back of his neck. His breath was coming fast and he held her close against him.

"Ilsa," he whispered, "I love you so."

"I'm glad, Terry, and I wish I could allow myself to love you as I did once. If only it weren't for . . . " She broke off and jammed her lips against his.

Snow continued to flutter against the windowpane and the fire crackled merrily on.

TERRY WATCHED ILSA as she sat before the mirror in her bedroom and applied cold cream to her face. She seemed very thoughtful, and he very much doubted if she had been listening to him at all. A little impatiently, he said,

"Did you get the instructions, Ilsa?"

"What instructions? Oh, yes. Yes, Terry dear, I got them."

"Repeat them then, so that I'll know you understand what you're to do and when you're to do it."

"Oh, it's just the usual routine. Go there, take off my dress, make the man take off his coat and then wait for the wife and the detectives. I've been through it a thousand times."

"I know, I know. But where, Ilsa—where and at what time?"

"Suite 1645 at the Broadway Hotel at ten o'clock tonight."

Terry heaved a sigh of relief. "Splendid. And what time are you to expect me and the boys?"

"Eh? Oh, ten-thirty or thereabouts."

"There won't be any thereabouts about it. We'll be there on the dot. After that, what, Ilsa?"

"After that? Why, nothing. Nothing happens after that, Terry."

"We're going places, Ilsa, after that. We'll take in a movie, a night club and then we'll think up something else to do."

"I'm through with movies and night clubs, Terry. And besides, tonight I'm coming straight home to wait for a telephone call from —from the man I love."

"Did he tell you he'd telephone from Chicago?"

"No, but I want to be here in case he does call. So, I'll say good night, Terry. And thanks for the assignment. Let me have some more, will you? I need the money so badly for a trousseau."

"You give me a severe pain in the . . ."

"I know I do, Terry. But this is love. Real love. Clean love. Something worthwhile."

"Yeah. So long." Before he lost his temper completely, Terry left the apartment and walked rapidly through the snow downtown. He was considerably worried. He had seen Ilsa through some strange phobias; but this was the strangest yet and he did not know what he could do about it. If only she had told him the name of the man she was interested in. Terry was a staunch believer that all was fair in love and war. And, God knew, he was in love with Ilsa. And since he was certain that she was in love with him, he thought it was up to him to protect her against herself.

He turned into a cafe and ordered a highball. Time ticked on, but his brain was still barren of ideas when it came time for him to leave.

AT THREE MINUTES to ten that evening, Ilsa turned into the lobby of the Broadway Hotel. A gorgeous mink coat, the collar of which was just flecked with snow, dropped almost to her ankles, and there were two or three fetching snowflakes on the veil of her jaunty little hat. She looked stunning, and more than one pair of male eyes followed her light and swinging step as she made her way unerringly towards the line of elevators. She stepped into the elevator and sat down on the new-looking old-fashioned seat.

"Sixteen, please," she said.

"Thank you, madame." That was part of the Broadway Hotel service, and one could always find it on the bill somewhere.

They did not have floor clerks at the Broadway. They were too embarrassing, and in one or two instances had proved too costly. Unchallenged, therefore, Ilsa made her way down the thickly-carpeted corridor until she found herself outside a door numbered 1645. Not without considerable boredom, she rapped with her neatly gloved knuckles. In due course, the door opened, the man stood back, and Ilsa passed into the gloom of the entrance hall.

"Please go right in," said the man. Ilsa went right in. Also she went white, and her heart took a flying leap into the back of her throat. "The bedroom," continued the man in matter-of-fact tones, "is through there, if you wish to disrobe."

Ilsa whirled about, her face ashen. "Arthur!" she said.

"Ilsa!" They gazed at each other as though both were coming slowly through a hypnotic trance.

"What in the world . . . " Ilsa could not say any more. She collapsed on a convenient chair and her head moved slowly from side to side in turgid confusion.

Arthur managed to recover himself. With quavering sterness, he said, "May I ask what you're doing here? I sent for a woman with

whom I was to be compromised. It's all very baffling."

Ilsa stood up dramatically. "Why should you want to be compromised?" she demanded. "You told me that you weren't married. You told me that you were going to Chicago to take care of some business matters. And then I find you here. Arthur . . . what is the meaning of this?"

"Before I answer you," replied Arthur stiffly, "suppose you tell me what you're doing here? You told me that you were a good woman. You told me that you had an independent income. And this is how you really make your money!"

"Why did you lie to me?" asked Ilsa quietly.

"I lied to you because I loved you," said Arthur sententiously. "You said that you loved me because I was different. You were flattered, so you told me, because you were the first woman in my life. I did not want to spoil your dream by telling you that I had been unhappily married for ten years. Why did you lie to me?"

"I lied to you," said Ilsa tearfully, "because I loved you, and I thought you were so good I didn't want to spoil it by letting you know the kind of life I've been forced to lead. It was a white lie, and I'm not ashamed of it."

"If yours was a white lie," said Arthur stiffly, "then mine was like the kind of snow you see in the movies."

"No, it wasn't. Yours was cruel. You misled me. You made me believe something that wasn't true."

"What about you?" demanded Arthur logically. "You made me believe that you were a lily, and now I find out that you're really a man-eating orchid."

"I've never eaten a man in my life," retorted Ilsa hotly.

"I was speaking metaphorically," said Arthur stiffly.

"Swearing at me isn't going to get you anywhere," said Ilsa.

"Let's change the subject," said Arthur irritably. "We're at crossed purposes. You can't see my point, and I can't see yours." He glanced at his wristwatch. "In the meantime," he suggested, "hadn't you better go into the bedroom and do whatever it is you have to do to compromise me? They'll be here shortly."

"Parade around half undressed in front of you?" squeaked Ilsa, with a rising inflection towards the end of the sentence. "I should say not!"

"You've done it in front of enough other men, haven't you?"

"That was different. That was business and entirely impersonal."

"Impersonal!" Arthur snorted with such vehemence he almost choked. "You expect me to believe that. A woman living the kind of life you've lived!"

"I don't expect you to believe anything," snapped Ilsa tartly. "But the day when you'll see me in anything but the fullest of clothing is so far away, you couldn't find it with a hundred inch telescope!"

"Who's swearing now?" crowed Arthur.

"I wasn't swearing," Ilsa told him indignantly.

"Oh, well, suppose you hop to it and earn your fifty dollars, or whatever it is you get for this kind of thing."

"I've just told you," said Ilsa with barbed patience, "that I'm not going to take off so much as an earring. As a matter of fact, I'm going."

She started for the door, and had almost reached it before Arthur flung himself in the path and brought her up short. "You won't reconsider?" he said.

"No. Certainly not."

"Suppose I force you?"

Ilsa's eyes widened. Curiously, she said, "And just how d'you propose doing that?"

Arthur grinned. "Something like this." He grabbed her and tried to tear the mink coat from her shoulders. A tightly-knotted calf-skin fist smashed into his face, and he reeled back. Ilsa stood with her back to the hallway leading to the door.

She said, "Try it again and see what you get. I know how to use my knees, too."

Arthur rubbed his chin reflectively. Then he came for her again. This time he succeeded in getting close enough to wrap his arms about her. Ilsa struggled, snapped at him with her teeth, and used her knees as though she were competing in a six days' bike race. She was getting altogether the worst of it, when the door opened and the room filled up with people. Arthur released her, and stood back. He was panting, and blood streamed from a deep scratch on his cheek.

TERRY'S MILD VOICE broke the tense silence. "Pretty," he admitted, "but hardly conclusive evidence of misconduct. Shall we come back a little later?"

"No," snapped Ilsa, adjusting her hat. "I'm going. Mr. Arthur Huntsman can get someone else to compromise him."

The woman who had accompanied Terry and his two men then stepped forward. She was not a very pleasant-looking woman, and one could have speared eels with the look she gave Ilsa. "How d'you know my husband's name?" she demanded. "I thought you were supposed to register as 'Mr. and Mrs. John Smith'?"

Ilsa laughed viciously. "Your husband," she said, "has been making love to me for the last month. But I give you my word I didn't expect to see him tonight. This was the first intimation that I had that he was married."

"Then what're you doing here?" asked Mrs. Huntsman with dangerous calm.

"That's my job. That's why I'm here. So that you can get the evidence against him for a divorce."

Terry was the only one who seemed to be enjoying the situation. He had strolled to the window and was now sitting on the radiator housing with a wide grin on his Celtic face. Mrs. Huntsman turned slowly to her husband.

"You rat," she said, and it is doubtful if any scientist could have infused any more venom into the two words. "And you knew it all along."

"I did not, Becky," he said. "I swear I didn't. I thought she was what she told me she was, and what I told you she was."

"You're a liar," said Mrs. Huntsman calmly. "I didn't mind divorcing you for awhile so that you could marry an heiress. God knows, we could do with the money. But a cheap little chiseler like this, nothing doing! Get your hat and coat. We're going."

Arthur expostulated, not however, altogether wholeheartedly, and it only took him a few seconds to gather together his things and to accompany his seething wife out of the suite. Terry's men stood about awkwardly. Terry got to his feet and tossed his cigarette into the empty fireplace. "Okay, fellows," he said. "That'll be all for tonight. Report at the office in the morning." The two men went out, leaving Ilsa and Terry alone.

"I'm going to crow," said Terry; "I'm going to crow like a rooster! Ilsa Mantell, ex-showgirl, ex-model, ex-this, ex-that, ex-Broadway-know-it-all fell for one of the oldest confidence games in the world. Such a good man—so clean, so kind and so gentle. Shut mah mouth!"

"When you're quite through," said Ilsa icily, "you can give me my fifty dollars, and I'll go home."

"But you haven't earned the fifty dollars," Terry reminded her. "You haven't even taken off your coat."

Ilsa tore off her hat and flung it across the room; she stripped off her coat and hurled it to the floor; her dress billowed about her ankles.

"Now," she yelled, "give me my fifty dollars and let me go!"

Terry put his arms about her and squeezed her into submission.

She never did get the fifty dollars, but as Mrs. Terence McCall, she now has a car, five charge accounts, and any time she undresses, she does it for the sheer hell of it. And when Terry bursts in on her, his attitude is anything but professional.

SINGLE ROOMS

By
CHLOE MADISON

FOR THE first time in—how long was it?—Phillipa Eaton entered her husband's room while he was dressing. He had just bathed. Rummaging through the big chest of drawers for his shorts, he stooped. His dressing gown slid open and disclosed lean, sinewy thighs. Phillipa sighed, trying to figure how long it was since she had last seen him like this.

"Roger," she called, "pardon the intrusion, but I wanted to remind you to dress for dinner."

"Ye gods!" he exploded. "A tux in this heat?"

"But Roger," Phillipa coaxed, tossing her pretty head sideways, "this dinner tonight is quite a stunt. Every woman in town is livid at not thinking of entertaining Shoot Higgins before me." She laughed. "But then, darling, I always do beat 'em to it, don't I?"

Roger growled unintelligibly. "You and these infernal parties! Well, it's the first time I ever dressed for a prize fighter, champion or no champion. I don't know what—" The remainder of his sentence was lost in a mumble.

Phillipa slid into a moire boudoir chair. The filmy rose chiffon of her negligee failed to cover the magnificent contours of her soft, gardenia-like flesh.

The ripeness of maturity but added loveliness to the great swelling of her breast, and her hips and thighs curved into tempting beauty. But her husband remained blind to temptation.

What ages it was, Phillipa reflected, since he had looked at her with anything approaching desire! Was this alluring body of hers always to be wasted? Oh, well! Perhaps it was her own fault! It was she who had insisted on the folly of separate rooms, after that first delightful year of their marriage. What a stupid move that had been! Modern, yes! The modern way of murdering marriage!

She studied Roger. He was still handsome. His brown hair waved back smoothly from a high intelligent forehead. His eyes, gray green, were deep set, and with a pang of self-pity she remembered the tenderness they had held but a few short years ago. His nose was patrician, and his jaw lean and splendid, but it was his mouth, that firm determined mouth that made her miserable now. She remembered the lavish kisses those chiseled lips had showered over her body. Ecstasy—burning, quivering ecstasy—those lips had shown her, but today? That mouth only snapped.

Heedless of her, Roger doffed his dressing gown. Rippling muscles played beneath the tan of his skin. A mad desire to touch him, running her hands through the curliness of that hair, overcame her. Weak and trembling with desire she called, "Roger!"

He turned irritably. "Now, what the hell is it?"

PHILLIPA STIFFENED. She felt the flow of hot, burning blood suffuse her face and neck. Rising, she glared at him.

"Even husbands can be polite!" Her voice was small and tense. Her tiny, smooth hands were clinched in a hard knot. The heavy lidded eyes flashed purple lights of anger.

Roger stared at her, interested. It was the first emotion she had displayed in a long time, barring the petty annoyances of social disappointments; or the petty elations of social successes. He had come to the conclusion several years ago, that instead of marrying a wife, he had married a social automaton. For love, after marriage, he'd had to look to the highways and byways. And they weren't so bad!

But this blazing fury before him was something different! He felt a frenzied urge to pick her up and crush those purpled lids—rip the tantalizing rose film from that luscious body and sample once again its perfumed delights!

Eyes agleam, he stepped toward her, but she eluded him.

"Dinner at eight, Roger!" she said primly. Once more her voice was wifely—and social. Roger swore as she stalked from the room.

Dressing for dinner, Phillipa struggled to repress tears of anger. How dare Roger act like this? Should she divorce him? His rudeness and indifference—how did they balance

against this comfortable home? Her staff of servants?

Caressingly, her hand traveled over the shimmering satin of her dinner gown. Only the most expensive modistes made possible such perfection of line. Her body was molded into devastating allure under the gleaming white fabric. Like a lover's embrace it hugged her throat, then surprisingly revealed the entire dimpling back. Over the rounded fullness of her breast, swooping in at the curve of her waist and flowing outward over the roundness of her hips and thighs the glistening satin delineated every breath-taking curve of her body.

Roger had paid for the gown. He would pay for many more. Wouldn't it be foolish to throw away such a meal ticket?

Dinner went off well. The women were all wild about Phillipa's find. Shoot turned out to be magnificently huge and virile. He towered over the other men present in length and breadth, and his features, though lacking the cultured finish of their husbands, had a distinct charm all of their own.

His unruly blond hair curled tightly, and his blue eyes had a boy's frankness. He grinned constantly and didn't look the least bit "rough" as one of the women remarked as they made their way to the terrace for drinks.

Over the champagne, his eyes sought repeatedly the heavy lidded ones of his hostess. There was child-like worship and more in them as he gazed at the raven hair sweeping back from her placid brow. Obviously she had captivated him, and her husband was the first to notice it.

Phillipa exalted in the coveting glances of her guest of honor and the jealous, annoyed ones of her husband. Daringly she invited the fighter to inspect her rose garden.

"Everyone else is familiar with it!" she laughed, rising from the wicker chair. "Come along, Mr. Higgins! This garden has won three consecutive prizes as the best in town. You see, I'm a champion too, in my way."

AWAY FROM THE terrace group, Shoot's fingers found the .tapering arm so close to him, and gripped it firmly.

"Yes, you're a champion, all right! Champion of beauty!"

Phillipa smiled up at him. "Why, Mr. Higgins! What a pretty speech! I didn't know fighters turned such pretty phrases!"

"No?" he retorted, grinning, "Well, turn in here, and I'll tell you some more."

They stopped at a rose covered arbor, safely guarded by the fragrant blooms from the questioning eyes on the terrace. Reaching for a cluster of the delicate pink flower, Phillipa tucked one in Shoot's lapel.

His big hand imprisoned her soft fingers as they lay on his chest. As his hold tightened, tremors of anticipation ran beneath Phillipa's milky flesh. Throwing back her head, she held up her lips, a flaming challenge.

Eagerly, Shoot covered the lush ripeness with his hungry mouth. His hand slipped around her waist and fondled her soft, rippling back.

The scene was wordless. A riot of long forgotten emotions clamored for fulfillment beneath Phillipa's fragrant flesh. Swaying in his arms, she felt her body melt as kisses pelted her eyes, the little hollows in her neck, the lobe of her ear. Gasping, they sank to the rustic seat and her head rested in the cavity of his shoulder.

Slowly his hand ventured under the satin opening at the back of her gown. It slid over the quivering flesh, seeking the warm enchantment of her heaving breast. Slowly, surely, his fingers massaged the smooth skin.

"Darling!" she moaned, "Kiss me! Kiss me!"

Shoot's embrace tightened. The enormous body nearly smothered her. She felt fire burn her lips to dryness. Finally, gasping for breath, she withdrew from the cloying embrace.

The sudden movement sent a cascade of satin falling from her shoulder. A glorious full, round breast was revealed to the silver moonlight!

Her hands clutched his curly hair, drawing him ever closer to her. "Darling—my darling—"

"YOU'RE SWELL! Swell!" Shoot murmured as Phillipa attempted to smooth her disheveled gown. His eyes were a caress.

She sighed. "Nice, nice boy! You've——Shoot, you've done things to me. You've made me live again, after three years! Oh!" Passion was in her voice now, and she clutched his hand tightly, "Dearest, must you go to Florida now? Tomorrow? Can't we keep on? I've just started to live! I'll—I'll—"

A kiss silenced her, and a tender hand quieted her trembling.

"Gee honey, I gotta go! I'm trainin' for the big fight. But listen kid—"

Shoot paused, studying the adoring upturned face.

"Shoot, what? Tell me, quick!" she begged.

"Well, I was wonderin' why you couldn't come along? Give up this palooka! You two was ready to quit before I came in the ring, wasn't you?"

Phillipa shivered. Go with him? Know always this mad exhilaration? Her breath came in quick gasps. In the throes of turbulent indecision her mind ran berserk. Quivers of delightful anticipation fought her reason. She struggled for mental balance.

Her house, her friends, her parties were fighting her body,.but the body won.

"When?" she gasped. "Shoot, when do you want me?"

"Tomorrow! We'll catch the four o'clock plane. You'll be mine, kid! All mine. We'll have a swell time. I'll show you real life. Gee, honey—" His lips found hers, sealing the contract.

Hugging their secret, they made their way back to the neglected guests. Roger acted the perfect host, but his eyes strayed amorously to the newly desirable wife. Having read the desire in Shoot's eyes, he, too, found this familiar creature devastating.

After the last guest departed, Phillipa eluded her husband and made for her room. Changing rapidly to a frilly negligee, she packed. Her body tingled as she stuffed layer after layer of dainty underwear into the bag. Her heart beat intolerably. She was going—going—giving up lots of things, yes! But he was worth it! An elopement? A divorce could follow later. What did it matter? To lose one moment of this glory was unthinkable.

A rap sounded on the door. Quickly she hid the bag under the taffeta flounce of the bedspread.

"Come in!" she called, breathless.

"Phillipa!" It was Roger. Miraculously, his eyes were tender. They gleamed with a coaxing fire, but Phillipa ignored them.

"Phil," he murmured. "I'd like to talk with you awhile. Are you busy?"

A pang of regret darted through her as she realized the desire in his eyes had come too late. Her body failed to respond. It was aching unbearably for the touch of her fighter-lover.

"I'm just going to take a bath, Roger," she replied nervously. "If it's important—"

"I'll be back in half an hour!"

When the door closed on him, Phillipa sank to the chaise lounge, trembling. She would have to prepare for the bad half hour that would be at hand when Roger returned. Should she tell him of her plans? She needed time to steel herself.

Another rap at the door. This time it was Jarvis, the butler.

"Mr. Higgins has just returned, Mrs. Eaton," he announced. "When he learned you'd retired, he begged not to disturb you, but asked me to give you this note, if your light was still on."

"Thanks, Jarvis."

A puzzled frown flitted over her satiny brow. Then, impulsively, she lifted the envelope to her lips.

As she read the contents a shiver traveled down her spine. Tears suddenly filled her eyes. Horrified, she studied the note.

"Filipa," she read, *"you was swele tonightt. I will lovve you forevor. But I changet my minde. Meat me at too insteade of fore, at the areport. Youre sweathert, Shoot."*

Crystal tears slid down her cheeks while peals of laughter cascaded from her ruby lips. Sobbing, she cried, "The ignoramus! Oh God! And I've have thrown up everything for him!"

Subsiding at last from the hysteria, she burned the incriminating note in the onyx fireplace. The last wisp of smoke was soaring upwards when Roger tapped at the door.

"Come in, dear," she called gaily, settling herself with catlike grace among the frilly pillows of the chaise lounge.

"Sweet!" he murmured, dropping to the floor beside her.

She smiled inquiry. "I thought you had something to tell me?" she asked.

Smiling fondly, he toyed with her ruby tipped hand.

"I have. Mrs. Eaton," he coaxed, "don't you think it's about time you became my wife again?"

His words unleashed a tempest beneath her ivory skin. Tremors of exultant joy soared through her being, as she gazed at those long lashed eyes, tender again, as early in their romance.

"What do you think of a little honeymoon?" he continued. "Lake George, or—"

His dressing gown slipped open, and gasping joyously, Phillipa's hands raced to his chest, burying themselves in the familiar curling hair.

(Please turn to page 64)

GIVE ME LOVE

By

FRITZI DUNN

"Just the mention of Kirk Duncan's name is enough to get a million feminine hearts fluttering," said Kitty.

THE girl with the strawberry lips paused in her manipulation of the switchboard plugs and stole a moment to gaze adoringly at Kirk Duncan. The little, round breasts that nestled beneath her cobweb brassiere rose and fell with ill-concealed emotion. Lights were flickering on her board. Reluctantly, she turned back to her mundane labors.

"Atlas Films, good morning. Mr. Wengart? One moment, please. Atlas Films, good morning. The Sales Department is located at 145 East 53d Street. Atlas Films, good morning. Sorry, Madam, but you'll have to write in for a photograph of Kirk Duncan. Atlas Films, good morning."

Kirk turned as he heard his name. The deep sombreness of his brown eyes—"soulful, searing orbs" the fan magazines called them—swept the reception room and came to light on the switchboard. A puzzled quirk played about his sensitive mouth. He walked back, leaned against the imitation mahogany wainscotting of the wall.

"Someone calling me, Miss?" he queried.

The girl with the strawberry lips looked up. Her eyes were bright stars of amazement. An excited pulse throbbed in her throat. Kirk Duncan had spoken to her! He was standing just two feet away from her, in the flesh!

"A call for me?" he repeated.

She forced a wan, nervous smile. "Y-y-yes, Mr. Duncan, b-but nothing important. J-j-just a woman asking for a p-p-picture."

Kirk grinned. "O. K., thanks a lot."

The girl with the strawberry lips watched him as he walked across the reception room and stepped into an elevator. His broad, sloping shoulders, narrow athletic hips and well shaped head thrilled her to the core. She sighed audibly, plugged in on an insistent outside call.

"Atlas Films, good morning. . . . "

KITTY BACON—the girl with the strawberry lips—slouched into the two room apartment she shared with Roberta—Bobby, for short—Meredith, tossed her hat and bag on the dresser and fell across the foot of a huge, double bed.

Bobby's auburn thatched head projected from a wide crack in the bathroom door.

"Hi, Kit!" she called.

Kitty waved her arm wearily. "Hello, Bobby."

A moment later, Bobby came into the bedroom, an all encompassing turkish towel wrapped around her midriff. A splendid bosom, a trifle too voluptuous, a bit too heavy, but none the less appealing, jutted from her upper torso with quivering enticement.

"A hard day?" she queried.

Kitty ran her hand across her brow. "Hard? Sister, it was terrific. Suddenly she sat up, eyes alight. "I forgot to tell you!" she cried. "Guess whom I saw?"

Bobby's round, blue eyes popped at the sudden outburst. "Er — er — Mahatma Ghandi!" she blurted.

Kitty slapped her. "Smart aleck! I saw Kirk Duncan! Not only that, but he *talked to me!*"

"No!" with pseudo-astonishment.

"Yes! He came up to the board and asked me whether there was a call for him. His voice is so deep and low and . . . and . . . thrilling!"

Bobby heaved her shoulders dramatically. "Like a ferryboat whistle, I guess."

Kitty fell back on the bed, gazing at the ceiling dreamily. "You're hopeless," she decided. "I don't think there's a spark of emotion in your whole body. Why, just the mention of Kirk Duncan's name is enough to get a million feminine hearts fluttering. Don't you realize he's the biggest thing in pictures today? I heard Mr. Wengart say he was a second Rudolph Valentino with a little bit of Wallace Reid and a touch of Lou Tellegen."

Bobby weaved the towel across her flat, boyish waist. "And a pinch of salt and three yards of bolonga and mix well and what have you got? Magnolia!" she cradled her breasts in the towel and wiped them gently. "I can't understand you, Kit. Here you've been working at Atlas for three years and the movie bug is still biting hunks out of your hide. Seems to me you'd be fed up with stars and stardust." She shook her head sadly. "Gee, I know I'm so sick of putting dresses on and taking 'em off that I'm thinking of joining a nudist colony."

Kitty snorted. "Modeling clothes is different. I don't see many of the players in the New York office. All of them are out West. Kirk Duncan just came in to make some personal appearances. He was up to talk to Mr. Wengart about it. He's so tall and broad-shouldered and his eyes are—"

Bobby stuffed the towel into Kitty's face. "Enough! Enough!" she shouted. "Let's rustle up some grub. I'm starved." She leaped out of range of Kitty's kicking feet. "I can't live on movie actors. I need good, solid food. Give me sirloin steak with onions anytime!"

Kitty's eyes closed. Her strawberry lips, the lower one drooping in a bee-stung pout, quivered.

"Give me love!" she murmured ecstatically.

KIRK DUNCAN stepped out of the elevator into the ornate lobby of the Allied Arts Building. The aspect of a "personal appearance" tour annoyed him. The very thought of a theatre full of gazelle-eyed women staring at him as though he were an apparition, was enough to give him the willies.

The one thing he yearned for most was the one thing his popularity denied him. One girl—a simple, plain girl—to call his own, was all he asked. A stenographer . . . a salesgirl . . . a telephone operator. Yes, the girl at the switchboard in the Atlas Films office. The girl with the strawberry lips. Just to have her alone, in some out-of-the-way place. That would be heaven.

Kirk shuddered and dashed for a taxicab as a crowd of women recognized him and called out his name.

"Any place!" he directed the driver. "The park!"

Riding in the cool, verdant quiet of the park, Kirk thought the whole thing out. One week from today he would be circling the big

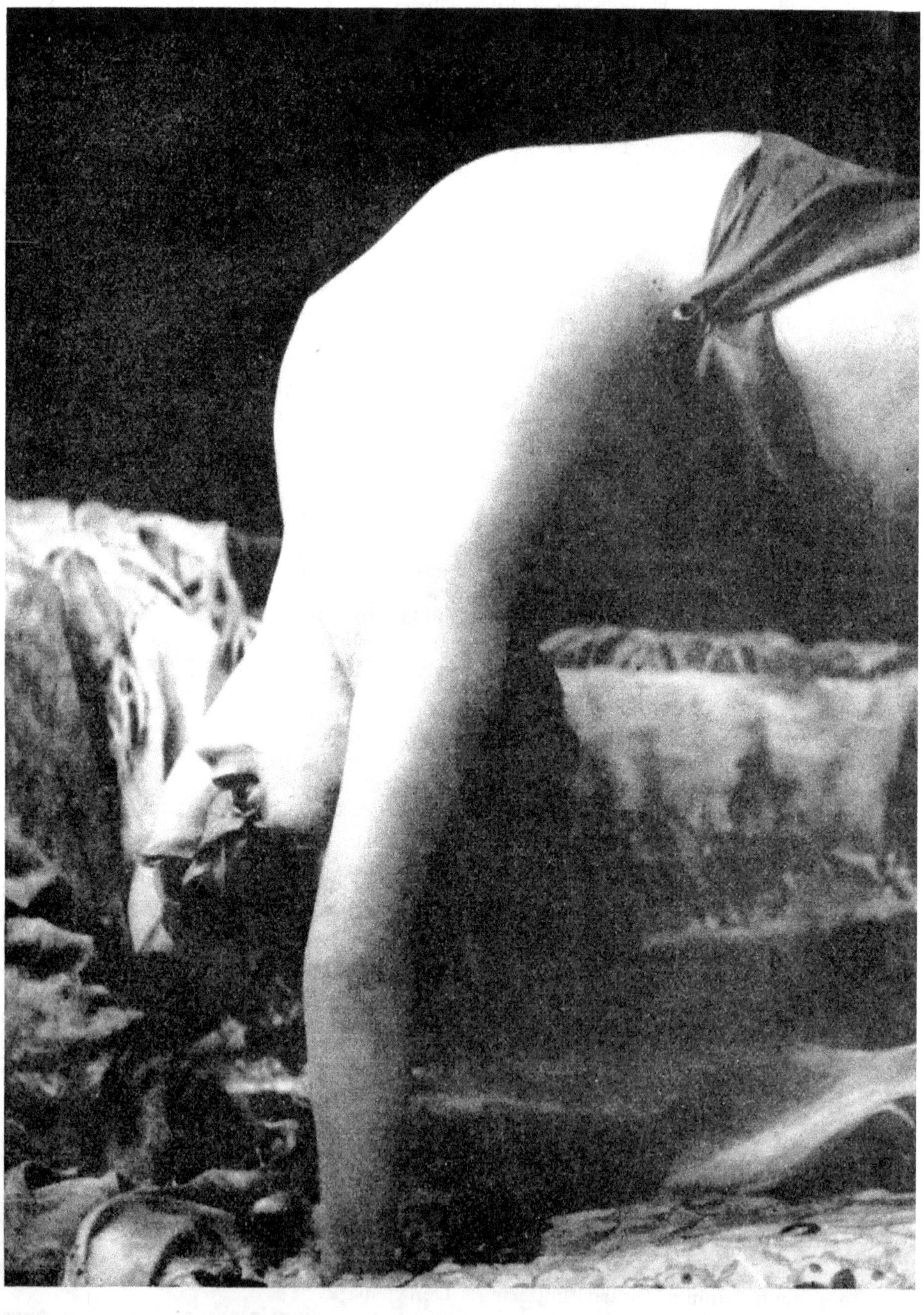

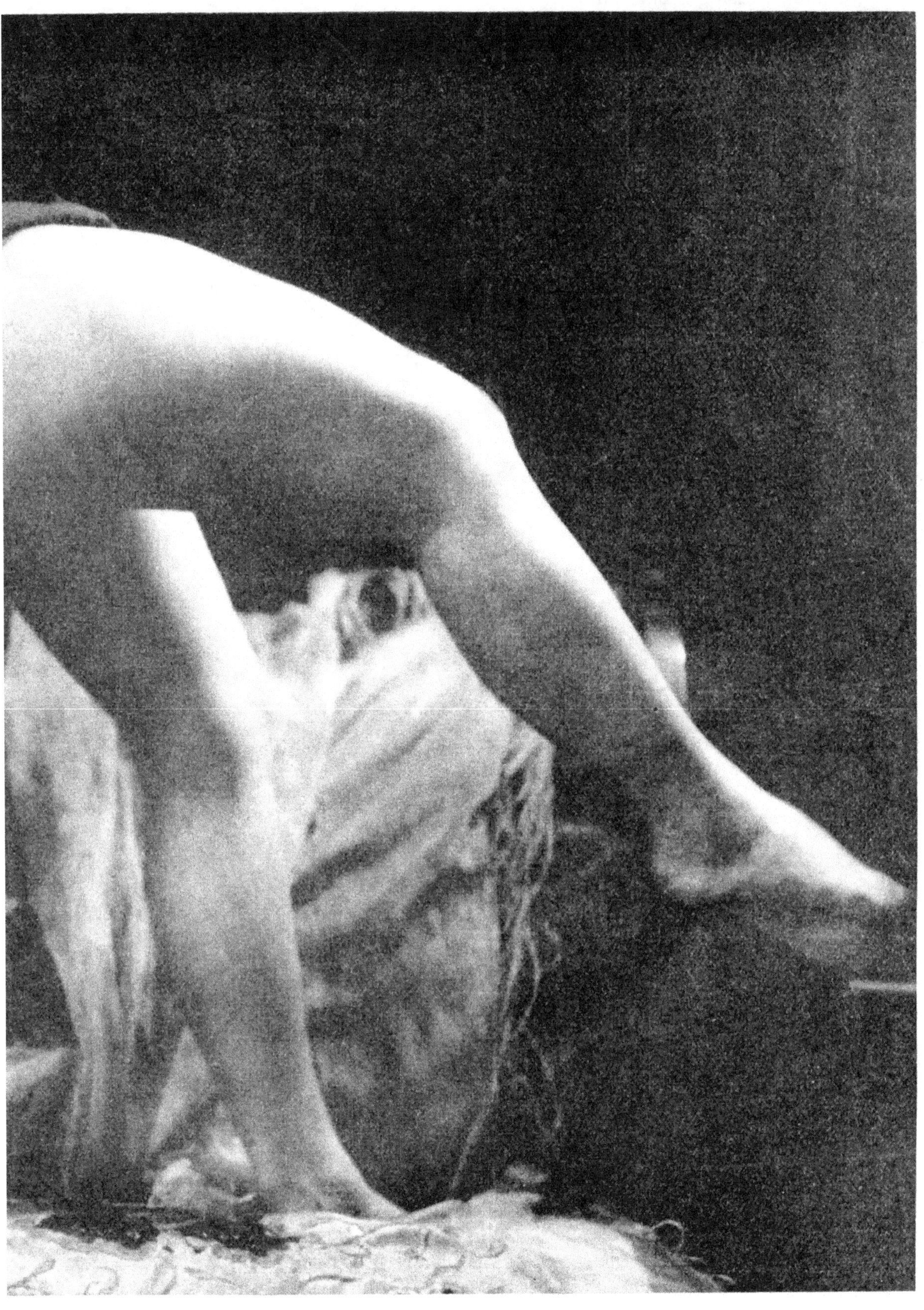

cities on his "tour". Women would applaud him, ogle him, storm his dressing room. Hundreds of them, thousands of them. His public! How he hated the term. His public!

If only he could get away for a breathing spell. Somewhere in the mountains where nobody had seen a moving picture since Mary Pickford's heyday. Just to live like a normal, human being for seven days would be heaven. He dug into his pocket and extracted a roll of bills. Excitedly he counted them. Eighty-four dollars. That would be more than enough. But what about clothes? Change of underwear? To hell with it! His handsome face beamed like a child's. Seven days of blissful peace! No fan magazine interviews! No publicity men! No pictures for the papers! No anything but himself!

Kitty sloshed through the soggy ground. She was miserable. What a black ending to her quest!

He leaned forward. "Grand Central Station!" he barked. "Hurry! I've got to catch a train!"

KITTY PROPPED the latest copy of *Movie Gossip* against the sugar bowl and settled down to her meal and "Kirk Duncan Tells the Story of His Love Life".

Bobby, on the other side of the table, snorted audibly. "Must you eat, sleep and drink that drivel?" she demanded.

"It says here," Kitty read, "that he was only in love once but that it was the greatest love of his career." She rolled her eyes passionately. "Oh, what a break that girl got."

"Break, my eye!" Bobby snapped. "Those heavy movie lovers are usually busts in a real boudoir. I wouldn't swap Mike, even if he is a taxi driver, for the best of them. Now, there's a guy who knows what it's all about."

Silence reigned for long moments.

Finally Kitty pushed her plate back, rose. She looked down at Bobby. Bobby looked at her. They both burst into laughter, coming around the table to meet each other and fall into each other's arms.

"Nuts, aren't we?" Bobby said.

"Worse than that," Kitty countered. "But, gee, Bobby, I can't help feeling the way I do about a man like Kirk Duncan. Every time I think about him my old heart goes loop-the-loop. You can call me a goose but it can't be helped."

The bell rang; three short, staccato blasts. Bobby jumped. "It's Mike!" she cried. "I have a date with him. Holy mackerel! Keep him busy while I dress, huh, Kitty?" She dashed into the bedroom, robe flying.

Mike was all smiles when Kitty opened the door and waved him in. He sailed his peaked cap into a chair and playfully pinched Kitty's cheek.

"Hot zam, did I have a famous fare today or didn't I?" he chortled. "And what a nut. He hops in the cab like a frightened rabbit, hollers for me to drive through the park, suddenly changes his mind when I'm in the park, yells for me to speed to Grand Central Station, slips me five bucks to buy him three pairs of socks and a suit of underwear, buys a ticket for a burg named *Loonerville* and hops the train before I can catch my breath."

Kitty listened with mild interest. Mike was always telling tales about his fares. "Who was it?" she questioned.

Mike grinned. "None other than Kirk Duncan!"

Kitty's lower jaw dropped. "K-Kirk Duncan!" she blubbered. "The—the movie actor?"

"Yep! In the flesh!"

Kitty's hands dropped to her lap. The right one had been holding the two sides of her silk negligee together. Mike gaped at the display of cute, slim-breasted nudity.

"Hey, button up, baby, or we'll all go to jail!" he cracked.

Kitty was oblivious to his remarks. Kirk Duncan going to *Loonerville!* Where was *Loonerville* and why was he going? She leaped up and ran for the bedroom.

"Bobby! Bobby!" she called.

Bobby, sensually attractive in a tight-fitting red satin dress, sat between Mike and Kitty and reviewed the entire story with calm detachment.

"Are you sure it was *Loonerville,* N. Y., Mike?" she questioned.

"Of course! Wasn't I standing next to him with his socks and underwear when he bought it? Seven bucks the ticket cost him and he peeled it off a roll that would choke a giraffe!"

Bobby turned to Kitty. "Are you sure your boss'll let you off?"

Kitty's hands fluttered excitedly. "S-sure! He s-said I could have my v-vacation either this week or next."

Bobby nodded. "All right, I'll call him in the morning and tell him you took ill and had to go to the mountains and that you're taking your vacation this week." Her eyes narrowed.

"Now listen. I think this whole idea is nuts, but since you're set on it, all right. There's only one warning. Don't throw yourself at his head too often because you're liable to get your own broken. Play the game the smart way. If he gets an inkling of who you are it'll be all off." She slapped her hand against Mike's thick thigh. "I tell you what. He'll probably fall for a smart society dame. Why not play it up? You're Marilyn Van Pell from now on, see? You—"

Kitty's lips trembled. "Yes, b-b-but supposing he knows M-Marilyn V-Van P-Pell?"

"He doesn't, you can be sure. Another thing. Make him come to you!"

Kitty was dizzy with instructions by the time Mike handed her back to a porter on the Eastern Express. Bobby stood on the station platform and waved.

"Don't forget," she called as the train moved out. "Get it in writing!"

THE EASTERN EXPRESS stopped at *Loonerville* with a derisive snort. Even the colored porter sniffed the dry night air of the sleepy town with palpable disdain, as he helped Kitty down and placed her bag beside her.

A rickety Ford station wagon seemed the only wheeled conveyance in sight. Kitty picked up her bag and approached it. The driver, dozing in the seat, lurched as she touched his elbow.

"Are there some hotels in town?" she queried.

He munched at a wisp of straw. "Well, there's the Beacon House," he drawled. "Feller come in on the 4:14 stoppin' there."

Kitty's heart leaped. "A-a man from—from the city?" she stammered.

"I reckon so, ma'am. Didn't have no baggage, though."

Kitty fought with the car door, swung it open. "Take me to the Beacon House," she directed.

In the privacy of a musty, oldish room, Kitty followed Bobby's instructions explicitly. She painted a dark crimson cupid's-bow on her lips, applied black mascara to her blonde eyelashes, blue shading to the lids.

Stripping off her traveling dress, a severely tailored gray drill outfit, she posed before the mirror, admiring the effect of her appearance in pink panties and a skimpy brassiere.

"No brassiere under any conditions!" Bobby had warned. "It's bad enough without one, let alone with one!"

Kitty removed the brassiere and permitted her small, pear-shaped breasts to swing free. They seemed to grow and develop out of confinement. She lifted them gently, conscious of the velvet texture of the taut skin.

"I don't think they're bad at all," she addressed her image in the glass. The image nodded in agreement!

Bobby had also warned against panties, but that was too much! After all, you couldn't throw yourself at a man! Or could you!

In place of removing them, Kitty hitched her panties up until the sheer glove silk clung to her thighs.

From her wardrobe bag she removed a light, fluffy dress, as gossamer a creation as she possessed. Even the bodice, although fashioned of more material than the balance of the gown, hardly obscured the pouting tilt of her bosom.

Five minutes with her ringlets of blonde hair and Kitty wasn't Kitty anymore! Proud of the transformation, she strutted before the mirror, hands on hips, lithe body swaying tantalizingly.

Kitty flashed the owner of the hotel a bright smile as she entered the lobby and approached the desk. "Good evening," she said, in the dulcet, bell-like voice Bobby had advised. "Have you any other guests at the present time?"

The oldster's Adam's apple bounced up and down his scrawny neck. "Yes'm, Miss Van Pell," he blurted. "'Nother gentleman from the city's stoppin' with us. He's gone fer a walk."

Kitty leaned over the desk. The neckline of her dress bellied out dangerously.

"What's his name?" she whispered.

The contents of her bodice were almost too much for the Beacon House proprietor's nerves. He blinked once or twice and moistened his dry lips.

"John Blake," he gulped.

A pang shot through Kitty's heart. Supposing it wasn't Kirk Duncan? Supposing it was all a grand mistake? Her knees felt weak.

"Here he is now," the proprietor said huskily.

Kitty turned to the door. It was no mistake! Kirk Duncan, in the flesh, was walking into the Beacon House! He looked at her as he walked by. He was even more handsome in gray slacks and a shirt open at the neck, than he had been in street clothes. His dark brown hair waved back from his forehead. His deep eyes shimmered under the light.

When he had turned the curve in the stairs and was gone, the proprietor nodded appreciatively. "Nice lookin' feller, Miss Van Pell, don'cha think?"

Kitty agreed.

The following morning, Kitty donned sweater and skirt and sallied forth. Kirk was tramping on the road, the proprietor informed her. She followed suit.

Almost a mile out of town, when Kitty was about to drop from sheer exhaustion, she spotted him, resting in the road. He nodded smilingly as she approached.

"You're stopping at the Beacon House, aren't you?" she queried.

He nodded, almost unwillingly. Looking up at her, the light of recognition illuminated his eyes.

"Yes," he said. "You're—"

"Marilyn Van Pell," Kitty supplied. "You've heard of my family, no doubt. I just sneaked away from society for a rest."

He crawled into his shell. Kitty prattled away, but all his answers were in monosyllables. Finally she suggested walking back. He rose.

Nearing town, Kitty decided to get under his reserve. "You know," she said airily, "you remind me of someone. I just can't place the person. What did you say your name was?"

"I didn't say, Miss Van Pell," he retorted, "but it's Blake. John Blake."

"Blake? Blake? Now let me see. Not the Blake's of Newport by any chance?"

"No, nor by any design. Just the plain Blakes of the United States."

His flippancy rankled Kitty, but she plodded on. "You're up here for a long stay?" she continued.

"No. I'm here for one short week. You see, I'm a sick man. I'm suffering from *magnorum feminarum.* It's a peculiar disease. You catch it from too many women."

Kitty's head jerked back. "I—I don't understand, Mr. Blake."

For the first time he looked at her and his eyes were smiling. "You wouldn't, Miss Van Pell," he said.

Five days and five nights of all the feminine wiles Kitty had at her disposal failed to make a dent in his protective armor. Fabulously untrue stories of her background, her social status and her wealth left him disinterested.

Sunday, the last day of his stay, dawned bright and cheerful. He had promised to hike

Kitty gasped. "You knew—knew me, all—all along?"

into the country with her. Maybe nature would conspire with her to make him warm up? Possibly . . . ?

Kitty slipped out of bed, spent a good half-hour with her effective facial disguise, donned a smart knitted outfit that clung to the curves of her figure close enough to reveal each hill and valley, and came down for breakfast. He was waiting in the lobby, smoking a pipe. He nodded as she bid him a cheery good morning.

"Ready for the hike?" Kitty queried, flashing a bright smile.

He looked up from a copy of the local paper. "Er—yes." He winced slightly at her carefully done hair, pencilled brows, mascaraed lashes and blood-red lips. "Are you?"

Kitty failed to get the implied sarcasm. "Surely," she replied. "I've been looking forward to it all night."

The sun beat down on the dusty road with all the hot, penetrating brilliance of mid-summer as they plodded away from the village.

Tiny beads of perspiration were beginning to form in the valley between Kitty's breasts. Evidently a knitted dress was a poor outfit for country hiking despite its advantages in other directions.

Kirk glanced at her at intervals, finally inquiring as to whether she was all right.

Kitty grinned. "A little hot. Couldn't we hike in a cooler place?"

He motioned to the woods flanking the sides of the road. "Would you like to go through the woods? Probably ruin your dress."

"I don't mind as long as it's cool."

He led the way, helping her over the embankment. Brambles caught at the hem of her skirt, ripped her sheer silk stockings, but she made no protest. The sun still filtered through the trees but most of its intensity was absorbed.

"Nice, isn't it?" he asked, waiting for her to navigate over a gnarled tree root.

Kitty lifted her dress above her knees and stepped across the obstruction. She hoped he noticed the flash of white thigh above her garter tops.

An hour later, he paused in a clearing. "Tired?"

Kitty's shoes were caked with mud and dry leaves. Her stockings were ruined. The hem of her dress had ripped out and now dangled haphazardly about her calves.

"A little," she whispered, patting her hair into place. As the words came out of her mouth, the patches of sky above them became dark and a crash of thunder split the heavens and rolled off into the valley.

"Rain!" Kirk said.

"Rain!" Kitty echoed.

It came, in great torrents, sooner than they expected. He took Kitty's hand and beat a hasty retreat to the road. In five minutes she was soaked to the skin, dripping with moisture. Her hair fell in a wet, soggy mass about her shoulders and her eyes became a black smudge from dripping mascara. Lightning flashed across the sky, followed by ominous peals of thunder. She clung to Kirk, really frightened.

"It must be at least a mile to the road," he said. "Think you can make it or shall I go back for raincoats and rubbers?"

Kitty held his arm. "P-please don't leave me," she whimpered.

He looked at her dress, sopping wet and clinging to her skin. It was as though she had no clothing on at all. Her breasts punched out with remarkable clarity.

"Come on," he urged. "I remember a cabin over beyond that pine grove. We can stay there until the storm blows over."

Kitty sloshed through the soggy ground. She was miserable. What a black ending to her quest! Tears formed in her eyes.

In the cabin, Kirk offered a clean handkerchief.

"Wipe your face," he said. "It's a mess!"

Kitty obeyed, removing all the mascara and carmine lipstick. The cabin shook with a tremendous crash of thunder. Frightened, she ran to him and threw her arms about his neck. He held her away and looked at her clean, fresh face. Recognition seemed to dawn in his eyes. He removed another handkerchief from his pocket and wiped the moisture from her throat and the upper curves of her breasts. His fingers brushed against her flesh. Kitty lurched towards him, twining her arms about his neck.

"I'm sorry, Miss Van Pell," he said quietly, "but you don't interest me that way. Of course, if you happened to be the girl with the strawberry lips at the Atlas Films switchboard—"

Kitty gasped. "You knew—knew me, all—all along?" she blurted.

He smiled. "Not until the rain ruined your makeup." Somehow the handkerchief he was using on her throat slipped into the billow-

(*Please turn to page* 64)

MOONLIGHT BAY

By
KAY CARROLL

AT A leisurely pace that fitted in with the mood of merry-makers seeking relaxation after a day's toil in the city, the excursion boat *Hiawatha* was ploughing its way one evening across Upper New York Bay.

The dance floor, a small enclosure set amidships, was scarcely big enough to accommodate the throng of couples who sought to keep in step with the rhythmic syncopation of an orchestra, and in the center of the shuffling crowd the riotous maze of fierily red curls on the hatless head of Tessy Shawn blazed like a beacon light.

"Get hot, Neil! . . . That's a swell number they're playing!" she murmured to her partner, the young man to whom she was tentatively affianced.

"It's not nice to dance so closely!" he replied, as he pressed her softly pliant body against him.

"We won't be conspicuous, darling, in this mob!" she smiled. "If you'll notice, everybody seems glued to somebody else."

"It isn't nice, just the same!" he asserted.

"Gee, you're a formal guy!" she said, acidly. "You dance like a stick or a pole or something."

"You're trying to dance like a postage stamp!" He frowned with a growing sense of irritation, although his sensations should have been entirely different, with Tessy snuggling in his arms.

"What's the matter with a stamp?" she countered. "It has its good points, sweetheart. . . . It sticks until it gets there."

"Always trying to wisecrack, aren't you?" he muttered.

She squeezed his hand. "Aw, Neil, don't be that way! . .. Come on and put a little pep into your steps."

"If you don't care for my style of dancing, then we'd better go up on deck and quit wasting time!" he stated, sullenly.

"Perhaps!" she said, smiling airily.

Immediately, he led her off the floor, up the stairs and out on the deck. The evening was balmy. A pleasant breeze flirted with the red curls about her ears and creased her chiffon dress so that the contours of her lissom body were etched in bold relief. Standing with her back to the rail on which her elbows rested, the tid-bits of her conical breasts jutted arrogantly as though they were challenging him to thrill them with a caress.

"Well, now that we're here, you might be allowed to put your arm around me!" she hinted.

He placed a hand most decorously at her waist.

Tessy sighed. "Is that the way you embrace a girl?"

"This isn't the place for an embrace!" he said, testily. "The deck is full of people."

"Yeah!" Tessy drawled. "I'll say it is! And everybody seems to be having a grand time except us."

His arm went a trifle further about her. . . . At the same time, his eyes glanced furtively to right and left.

"Don't be scared, darling!" she laughed. "The trouble with you is that you think everybody is staring at you all the time. . . . As a matter of fact, nobody is paying the slightest attention to you. . . . You're too self-conscious!"

"I didn't bring you on this trip to be lectured!" he growled.

"I'm sorry!" she murmured "Give me a kiss."

His lips swooped toward her pretty face, smacked a swift kiss and retreated, ignoring the salient fact that her luscious lips were parted invitingly.

"And that's a kiss!" She laughed sardonically.

"Tessy . . . we're out on an open deck . . . you don't want to make a show of yourself and me, do you?" he remonstrated.

"Oh, don't be silly!" She looked around the deck. "Take a squint at all those other loving couples . . . do you think they're making a show of themselves?"

Neil turned his head. . . . The first couple his glance encountered were seated in a deck chair, and their lips were clinging together moistly. . . . He looked at another couple, standing at the rail only a few feet away, arms entwined about each other, male fingers

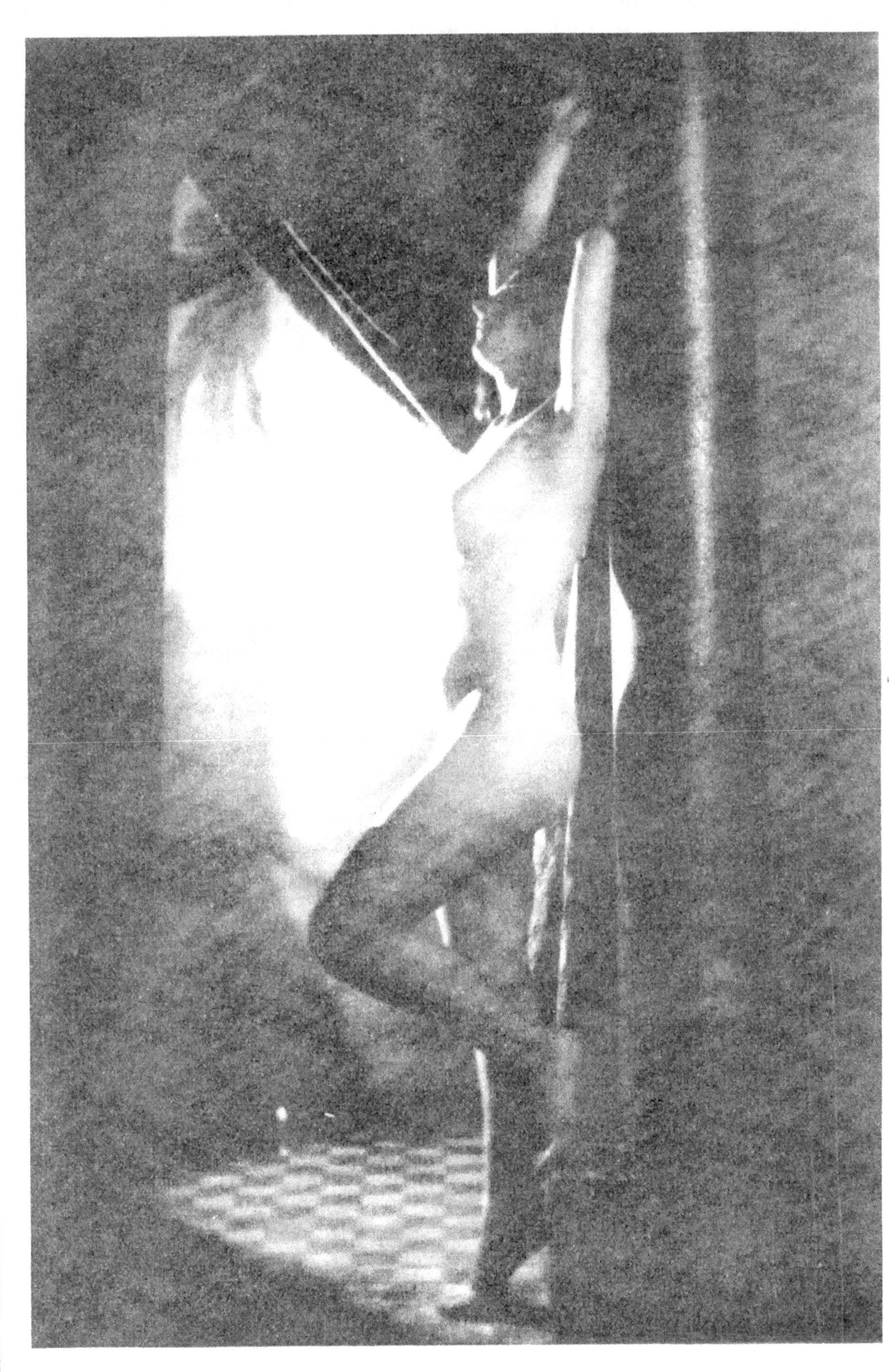

reveling in the drooping softness of an unbrassiered breast.

"Huh!" he said. "Sure they're making a show!"

"Right now, they don't realize that anybody else is living but them, darling!" Tessy frisked a curl. "I don't think you like me very much, Neil."

"Why?" he exploded. "Because I don't paw and maul you and kiss you in public?"

"A little affection wouldn't harm you!" she murmured.

"After we're married . . ."

Her laughter cut his sentence short. "Oh, yes! After the wedding ceremony you're going to swamp me in love! And everything is going to happen *'after we're married'*. . . . Can't we have a little fun before?"

He stared at her exasperatedly. "You don't understand."

"Maybe I don't." She turned away from him. "I guess I'll go down to the ladies' room and powder my nose. . . . Wait for me here."

Her sinuous hips weaved along the deck. . . . Neil watched her until she vanished. . . . Then he heaved a sigh, gazing out to sea.

TESSY'S THOUGHTS WERE peppery as she scampered down the stairs.

"That guy needs a shot of something to wake him up!" she murmured. "That would be my luck . . . falling in love with a fellow who is nothing but a cold potato."

Many were the boy friends that she had taken on probation since her high school days. . . . Neil was the only one she had ever considered in a serious way. . . . She had dreamed of the time when they would settle down to housekeeping in a little apartment, where her days would be filled with plans for him, and her nights would be throbbing with the sweet ecstasy of passionate love. . . . But he seemed to be lacking in the spark of physical fire that was the very breath of life to her!

A carmine lipstick was being touched to a juicily red mouth which really needed no cosmetics when she heard a voice behind her:

"Tessy!"

She shot a glance over her shoulder, then gasped:

"Miriam, darling! . . . Of all people!"

An olive-skinned brunette, with big lustrous black eyes and poutingly full lips, smiled at her. "I'm certainly glad to see you again."

"When did you get back to New York?" Tessy kissed her.

"Just a trip for a few days!" replied Miriam. "We're going back to Boston on Saturday."

"We?" echoed Tessy.

"Meaning my husband and me!"

"Oh, did you get married?"

"Sure! I wrote you about it, but the letter came back. I guess you must've moved."

"Who's the lucky fellow? Did you meet him in New York?"

"No, I met him in Boston, but he used to live in New York. . . . Name is Leonard Bates."

For a fraction of a second, the lipstick in Tessy's hand ceased its painting, her eyelids blinked twice, then she murmured:

"Good luck! . . . I hope you're very happy."

"We get along swell, Len and I!" declared Miriam. "Who're you with tonight?"

"The latest boy friend!" smiled Tessy.

"Serious-minded this time?"

"Yes and no!"

"Can't make up your mind, huh?" Miriam laughed. "But I'll bet he thinks you're the grandest thing."

"He says so, but he has a funny way of showing it!" Tessy put away her lipstick and snapped her handbag shut. "You'd think that a fellow who's crazy about a girl would enjoy a little loving once in a while!"

"Maybe he's bashful!" said Miriam, giggling. "Some guys are a bit backward about coming forward . . . if you know what I mean."

"Naw!" Tessy sighed. "It isn't that! He's got a bad case of the *'shouldn'ts'* and the *'don'ts'* . . . you know . . . we shouldn't do this and we oughtn't do that, it isn't nice to pet and kiss . . . and so forth." She wrinkled her little nose. "He says all such things should wait until we're married."

"I guess he's afraid to trust himself!" murmured Miriam. "If I were a fellow, I'm positive that one kiss from those juicy lips of yours would make me want to go much further than that."

"Nobody's stopping him!" smiled Tessy. "After all, innocence is something you'll find only in the dictionary these days."

Miriam linked arms with her. "Come on upstairs and let me introduce you to Len. . . . I'd like to meet your boy friend, too."

IT WASN'T LONG thereafter that Tessy was gliding about the dance floor with Leonard Bates. Sparks of excitement were shining in

her eyes, and her breath fanned his cheek in warmly recurrent zephyrs.

"You certainly put *that* over great!" he said. "Nobody could tell, when Miriam introduced us, that we had ever seen each other before that minute. . . . *'How-do-you-do?'* you said, real society-like." He chuckled and brought her closer into him.

"You weren't so bad yourself, Len, old boy!" she smiled. "I had warning, because Miriam told me your name when she broke the news of her marriage. . . . But you hadn't the faintest idea I was on the boat until you saw us together. . . . *'Pleased-to-meet-you!'* . . . And you said it without batting an eyelash."

Their laughter mingled gaily.

"Where did you and Miriam get so well acquainted?" he asked.

"We used to work in the same department at Rumpel's store, and we got very friendly." Tessy paused significantly, then remarked:

"You picked yourself a hot baby, didn't you?"

"Might as well, while the picking's good." His arm coiled tighter about her. "But I can remember the time when I thought they couldn't come any hotter than you, beautiful."

Tessy laughed softly. "Did Miriam cause you to change your mind?"

"No!" he replied, promptly. "I still think you're a ball of fire." His arm dropped low, his fingers spread fanwise until he felt the firm jelly of a hip. "But you wouldn't marry me . . . and . . . what's a fellow to do?"

"The next best thing, I guess!" she murmured.

"That's what I did!" he rejoined.

Cheek to cheek they were dancing now and with every step it became more intimate, until hip fitted hip and thigh met thigh. . . . The floor was excessively crowded. . . . They could only move very slowly, and the orchestra was timing its syncopation accordingly.

"Do your stuff, kid, like old times!" he breathed in her ear, his lips brushing a red curl.

Tessy's hips undulated maddeningly, in a slow-motion cadence.

"Is that what you mean?" she whispered, her breasts almost flattened on his chest.

"Oh, girlie, girlie!" His voice was husky. "Do that again."

"Len," she said, "let's go up on deck where we can be alone."

There weren't many unoccupied spots on the deck. . . . Most of the available nooks were already taken. . . . But Tessy, with the eye of an eagle and the fiery temperament which, once aroused, would not be denied, spied a cozy corner, and there she drew Leonard.

"This *is* like old times!" he grinned, sitting on a conveniently coiled mound of rope, and pulling her down on his lap. "Kiss me, redhead, and make it hot!"

"L-e-n!" she moaned, her parted lips burrowing into his mouth. "You're a gift from heaven. . . . Gee, tonight of all nights . . . how I need you!"

Leonard couldn't reply. His mouth was completely filled by the fury of her kiss!

WHEN TESSY GLADLY accepted Leonard's invitation to dance, Miriam had stayed on deck with Neil, who found a chair for her, and, at her suggestion, placed it in the shadows beneath an overhanging lifeboat. Seating herself, she said:

"Aren't you going to get yourself a chair?"

"I couldn't find another vacant one!" he replied.

"Then share this with me!" She edged over to make room for him.

"Oh, I'm okay!" he said. "Don't bother. . . . You'll only be making it uncomfortable for yourself."

"No, no!" she exclaimed. "This chair is plenty big enough for two people. . . . I'm not quite as fat as all that."

Of course, she expected a complimentary rejoinder, but Neil wasn't the type given to the repartee of flirtation. . . . He simply smiled and lit a cigarette.

"May I have one?" She caught his hand and pulled him toward her. "Please sit down!"

Neil sat on the extreme edge, but she yanked him closer. "Oh, don't be afraid of me. . . . I'm not exactly poisonous."

He flushed red in the dim shadows. . . . Now his leg was pressing very intimately against a soft thigh and softer hips that were clothed only in the flimsy silkiness of a dress which permitted the subtle warmth of lush femininity to seep through. . . . Neil was conscious of the fact that it was a pleasant sensation!

She plucked the cigarette from between his lips and put it in her own pouting mouth, first wetting its tip with a pointed tongue that flicked it expertly. "If you don't mind, I'll take this. . . . You can light another for yourself."

"Yes . . . of course . . . that's all right!" he stammered.

Miriam smiled. . . . It was a bit of a thrill for her to encounter a good looking young man who wasn't bending all his energies toward turning a chance acquaintanceship into an orgy of intimacy. . . . Neil was the first fellow she could remember who didn't try to "*make*" her. . . . And male instincts being what they are, she was accustomed to getting plenty of attention!

"Wonderful night, isn't it?" she murmured.

"Yes . . . it's great!" he replied.

"Look at that moon on the bay!" she continued. "They ought to call it Moonlight Bay."

He grinned. "Yeah . . . it's pretty."

But the way he said it indicated that moonlight bay was only a moon shining on the water, nothing more and nothing less, and it wasn't anything to get excited about. . . . Her passionate soul, ever on the alert for romantic situations, resented the implication in his tone. . . . Here was a handsome young chap, sitting alone with her in a spot where *anything* could be said and *anything* could be done, and his attitude was as unresponsive as a chilly, distant ice-berg! . . . Usually, it was the man who started a hectic assault on her charms, and it was she who was on the defensive!

"I can't be losing my sex-appeal!" she thought. "Something has to be done about this."

Amid a cloud of cigarette smoke that enhanced the sensuousness of her lips, she murmured:

"When a fellow and a girl are looking at a gorgeous moon, at least he ought to be holding her hand, don't you think?" She laid her warm fingers on his twiningly.

"And I think he might even put his arm around her . . . if she's willing!" she added, smiling as she guided his hand to her waist and pulled his arm until it circled her so completely that his fingers were resting on the softness of an uncorseted torso.

"I'm willing!" she whispered. "Did it ever occur to you that the *man-in-the-moon* means much more to a girl when a nice boy is with her?"

Neil's pulse was doing a trip-hammer beat. . . . Furtively, he glanced around him. . . . There were other couples, dimly outlined, here and there, but they were too engrossed in each other to notice anything but themselves.

His eyes burned feverishly, his lips felt hot and dry. . . . He looked at Miriam, nestling there in the hollow of his arm. . . . Straining against the texture of her dress, luscious breasts thrust themselves toward him as if they were defying him to resist their compelling appeal. . . . If he was to move his hand only a few inches upward. . . .

"Don't be bashful!" he heard her say. "A moon, a boy, a girl . . . only one thing more is needed to make it a heavenly combination, and that's a kiss."

She laid red dark head on his shoulder. . . . Her pouting lips fell apart. Her hand crept to his head, slowly bringing his face to hers until their lips met, and every nerve in his body tingled as he tasted the cloying honey of her mouth.

With a gasp, he wrung his lips away from her clinging kiss.

"We shouldn't . . . act like this . . . suppose Tessy . . . your husband . . ." He was stammering almost incoherently.

Miriam laughed. She couldn't remember when she had enjoyed such a thrilling moment.

"You should worry, darling boy!" she whispered. "Life is nothing but a gamble, so take a chance!"

Her tenuous fingers flitted over him. "Quick!" She pulled him deeper into the shadows. "You may never have another opportunity like this!"

Neil groaned and shuddered. . . . A passing ship gave a long, wailing blast of its siren. . . . He didn't even hear it!

IT WAS NEARLY midnight when Neil stood with Tessy in the hallway of an apartment house uptown.

"I'd invite you in, darling, but it's rather late!" she smiled. "I had a wonderful time tonight. . . . Did you?"

"Swell!" he grinned, both arms hugging her. "We ought to take those boat rides more often."

"Sure!" she agreed "See you tomorrow. . . . good night!"

She raised her lips for the usual placid kiss that he implanted . . . But there was nothing placid about it. . . . Under the thirsty impact of his lips her mouth fell open, and for a throbbing minute they stood in a trance.

"Neil!" she gasped, breathlessly. "I thought you didn't like to kiss like that . . . have you been kidding me all this while?"

"I've changed my mind, sweetheart!" he

(*Please turn to page* 64)

GYPSY

. . . A woman with flashing black eyes rose from the happy circle, leaped into the firelight, and began to dance.

By
FRANK KENNETH YOUNG

NEAL'S CAR slipped smoothly through the scented purple dusk. Its high-powered motor, throttled down to minimum speed, purred with mechanical contentment. Its powerful lights cut a path of diffused radiance as mellow and soothing as moonlight.

Neal lolled lazily behind the wheel. He was bareheaded, his wavy brown locks ruffled by the stirring breeze. The open collar of his soft white shirt lay back, revealing a muscular, sun-tanned neck. The bare arms resting upon the wheel were brawny and brown. Half-closed eyes watched the road perfunctorily, but the mind behind them was dreaming. The soul was drifting far afield. . . .

It was a pretty night, a night for languorous love and exotic adventure. Yet the seat beside Neal was empty, and he had no date. He had quarreled with his wife, and forsaken her society for the peaceful quiet of a country road. It was much pleasanter here under the stars than in a stuffy apartment. Yet he sighed, conscious of a subtle yearning for feminine companionship. . . .

FIDDLES

The car rounded a curve in the road, and began coasting down a long decline. Neal's ears were pricked by enchanting sounds—long-drawn wailing and high treble notes, all harmoniously blended. It was like the music of gypsy fiddles! He roused to alert attention, his keen gaze sweeping both sides of the road.

Through a copse of boxelder and briar, he saw the fitful gleam of the flickering camp-

fire, the dark shadows of wagons and tents. Slipping down into the dusky valley, he was given full view of the picturesque scene. The sight was one to gladden one's eyes, and the wailing of the fiddles was doubly distinct.

Here, in a grassy clearing beside the road, the nomads had pitched their camp for the night. Their gayly decorated wagons and house cars were drawn up in circular formation about the fire. Dogs and horses, tethered to the vehicles, dozed and drowsed among the shadows. And in the circle of light cast by the flickering flames, the party of gypsies was gathered.

Lured by the colorful scene, Neal stopped his car beside the road, just behind a fringe of trees. From this point of vantage, he could see without being seen, and listen to the wild, barbaric music that throbbed upon the night air. He could even see the fiddlers, in their gay blouses and wide-rimmed, black hats, bodies swaying rhythmically to the melody as they played.

What a pleasant life. Joyous, carefree, spiced by romantic adventure, and ever haunted by the call of the beckoning road. For the moment, Neal wished desperately that he were a gypsy, a victim of vagabondia!

Then he sat up with a start, as a woman rose from the happy circle, leaped into the firelight, and began to dance. At the distance, Neal could not see her glossy, black hair, flashing eyes and laughing lips; but not even distance could blur the passionate movements of her dance. Not even her barbaric costume could quite conceal the beauty of her lithe, slender body. Neal was thrilled by the promise of entertainment both exotic and bizarre.

Wilder, more abandoned, became the fiddling; louder and faster grew the music and the rhythm. And some of the passionate beauty of the dance, and the tumultuous spirit of it, entered into Neal's blood, rousing his emotions and bringing a faint flush to his cheeks. He leaned forward, breathing excitedly, his burning gaze trained intently upon the leaping, whirling figure. So intent was he in absorbing every movement that he quite lost himself in contemplation.

He was first made aware of a third presence only when the nearby bushes were parted, and a woman stepped quietly to the side of the car. He gave a start as he heard her voice, low, sweet and musical, murmuring amusedly:

"Then you are the owner of this land, that you watch us so closely?" The woman paused, gazing impudently up at him.

"Good Lord, no!" he hastily disclaimed. "I didn't mean to spy, if that's what you mean! I was attracted by the music, and tempted by the dancing."

"You like it?—the music, the dancing?" she inquired interestedly.

"Oh, it's swell!" he said warmly. "Those fiddles!—there's something in their tones that thrills me! In my opinion, there's nothing more beautiful than gyspy music.

"What of the women?" she asked slyly.

"Women, too, are like melodies," he answered. "Filled with life, color, and rhythm!"

And then, because he was a woman-loving man, he became more keenly alive to her, and to her fascinating appearance.

Her lustrous black hair was loosely waved, tumbling abandonedly about her ears, and gathered in wide braids that hung down over her shoulders. Her eyes, unusually large and as deeply black as midnight, were fringed with curling lashes that swept her dusky cheeks. Even, white teeth were revealed by full, red lips, exquisitely chiseled, curved back in a teasing smile.

Neal swallowed nervously. "Are you—er —traveling with them?" he asked, nodding toward the group about the fire.

"But yes," she assured him. "I am Zola, the daughter of King Rom. Tonight, I grow weary of the fiddles, and steal away by myself to dream. I see the lights of your car, and find you here. It is nice—no?"

"Very!" he said gravely. "But not nicer than you!"

She chuckled appreciatively. Her eyes, like dark stars, glowed through the dusk, with a light of lure in their depths.

Not even the dusk could conceal the wild, vivid beauty of her face; if anything, it rendered it doubly attractive. Neal could even see the long, narrow V of smooth flesh that dipped deep into the front of her low-cut waist. Softly rounded bulges in the cloth on both sides of the V indicated her womanly bosom, giving an impression of delightful warmth and voluptuousness.

Quite likely, she observed Neal's interest. "My heart!" she murmured, pressing a palm to the mound of one luscious breast, "it grows lonely—for love!" She gazed up from dark, inscrutable eyes, as though expecting him to understand.

He did! "Would you like to go for a ride?" he asked. "I've got nothing else to do. We might take a spin around and be back before your absence was noticed."

"How strange!" she murmured. "Most people of the towns, they order us to move on; they set their dogs on us! And you ask me to ride with you! Me—Zola!—a gypsy!"

Neal flushed. "Don't feel like that!" he said hastily. "You've got the wrong impression. I invited you because I like and admire you. I'm not like those other people. If they knew you, they wouldn't treat you so shabbily, either!"

"So?" she smiled.

"Come along!" he said simply, opening the door of the car, and reaching a hand to help her.

A tingling thrill ran through him as he felt her cool, soft fingers in his grasp. She stepped upon the running board of the car and leaned forward, and the loose front of her waist bulged, with the weight of her breasts against it. Neal thrilled again as he glimpsed the deep, shadow-filled valley. Then she was seated beside him, her face radiating the pleasure of her soul.

He closed the door softly, pressed the starter, and nosed the car out into the road. The next moment, they were slipping smoothly away from the gypsy camp, and the wailing of the fiddles was growing ever fainter in the distance. . . .

It was a pretty night. Blue sky was dotted with twinkling stars. A thin sliver of moon lounged lazily upon a fleecy couch. A balmy night breeze was heavy with summer fragrance. The long, brown road a twisting ribbon of allure, stretched away into the country. . . .

When not watching the long, brown ribbon of road, Neal gazed deliberately at his dusky companion, and was ever more favorably impressed by her exotic appearance.

Bracelets, rings, ear-rings, and other gaudy

ful a night. But it is more pleasant to ride with so handsome a young man!"

"Thanks!" laughed Neal. "Glad if you like my looks. Words can't express my admiration for you!"

She seemed to nestle closer to him. "Do you always express those things in words?" she whispered seductively.

Neal thrilled warmly. Hesitated. Then swerved the car to one side of the road, and stopped. "Zola!" he murmured, turning toward her.

Eagerly, she waited; expectantly, she stared; red lips parted, dark eyes glowing. Her luscious breasts rose and fell as though moved by inner emotion.

adornments—all lent color and charm to her already barbaric beauty. Her dusky skin, black eyes and red lips were made more arresting by the vivid colors of her clothes. The slight jolting of the car caused her breasts to bob and tremble; the thin material of her dress to hug her beautifully arched thighs.

Neal saw that her calves and ankles were bare, her feet encased in dainty slippers with

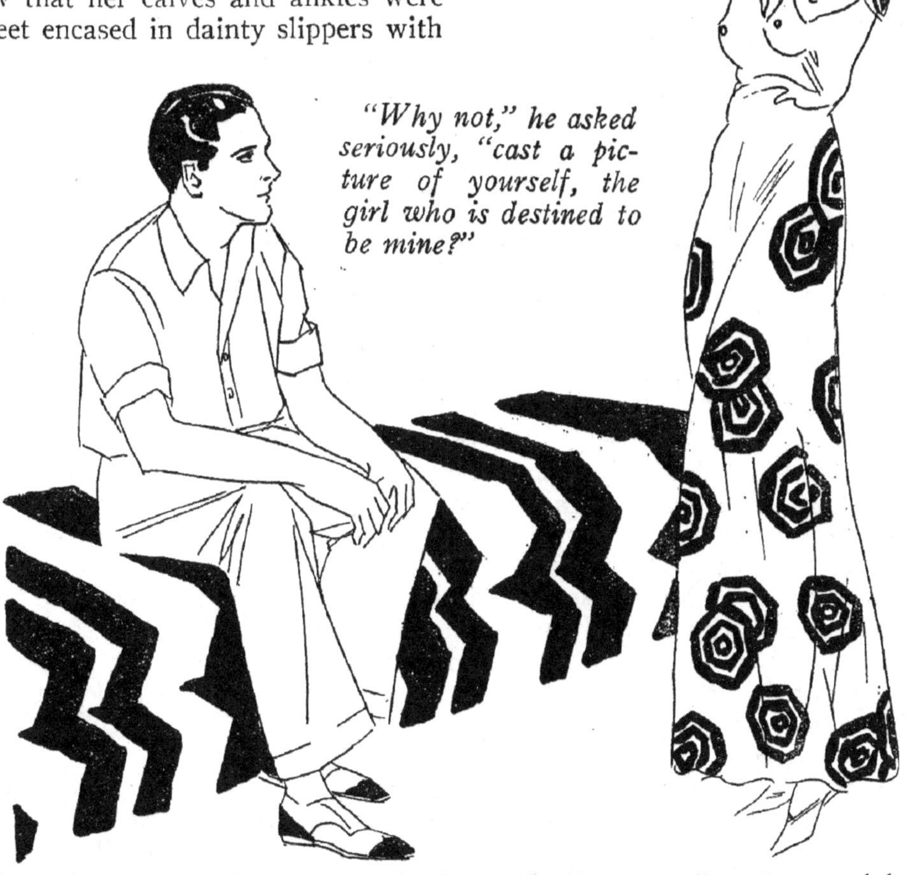

"Why not," he asked seriously, "cast a picture of yourself, the girl who is destined to be mine?"

red high heels and narrow straps buckled across her insteps. Raising her eyes, he found her regarding him.

"Glad you came?" he asked smilingly.

She nodded vigorously. "It is pleasant," she said, "to ride in the evening, on so beautiful a night.

Neal's arms slipped around her and drew her to him. He felt the yielding of her undulating waist, the pressure of her soft shoulder against his chest, the touch of her voluptuously rounded hip. Her wavy hair was a dark fluff before him, obscuring his vision; her subtle fragrance was as a delightful drug. Impulsively, he tensed his arms, enclosing her in a crushing embrace.

"You're sweet!" he whispered. "You're beautiful! You're tender, and warm, and wild—like those fiddles! You stir my blood and cause my nerves to tingle with excitement!"

She nodded understandingly, and slipped her round, bare arms about his neck. She turned so that she was facing him, and pressed her resilient breasts firmly to his chest. He grew warm and thrilled to their intimate contact. Then her fingers interlocked behind his head, drawing his lips down to meet hers.

He closed hungrily over the soft, ripe petals, delighting in their moist sweetness, their eager warmth. His arms crushed her more passionately, until he felt her heart beating tumultuously against his own, her body tensing with emotion. For a brief moment, he knew rapturous ecstasy; and because she responded so willingly, the kiss was repeated and prolonged. . . .

It was a bewitching night. The sky was so high and blue, the stars so warmly twinkling! Even the balmy breeze seemed to sigh faintly away, leaving only a breathless hush, an exquisite interval. . . .

When, finally, Neal released the girl's lips temporarily, she relaxed limply against him, and expelled her breath in a long, tremulous sigh. Her dusky cheeks were pale; her large, dark eyes alight with love.

"You are a man!" she said simply. "Your kisses do to my soul what food does to my body when I am hungry. You fill me completely with all I've been longing for!"

Neal grinned happily and dropped a hand upon her rounded knee. She did not demur. Somehow, under his nervously moving fingers, the hem of her dress crept upward, and his palm contacted bare flesh with skin as soft and smooth as velvet. She stirred faintly and smiled.

"Zola!" he whispered, "I'm mad about you!"

"My dear," she answered, pressing the hand that rested upon her leg. "Let us return to the camp. I have a tent all my own. Will you come with me?"

"Your father—or your brothers—?" he said dubiously.

"Will be asleep by now. They will not see us when we come."

"All right."

He pressed another fiery kiss to her sweet lips, then started the car and turned it back toward the gypsy camp. The return ride was made in silence, and they arrived athrill with anticipation.

But the fiddles were still now. Members of the camp had sought their rest. The campfire had burned down and died. Only where the dogs and horses were tethered could be seen an occasional sign of life or wakefulness. . . .

NEAL PARKED HIS car among the bushes, and helped Zola to alight. Together, her hand clasped warmly in his, they crept through the dark to the privacy of her tent. She entered before him, holding back the canvas flap, that he might follow.

He stood in the warm, sweet-smelling interior, and waited till she made a light. Then she urged him to be seated upon a low couch, and she sat down beside him. Again they embraced and kissed. His hands caressed her, and she shivered from sheer ecstasy.

"Would you," she breathed, insinuating herself into his arms, "wish me to tell you of the future? It is an ancient custom among my people."

"Tell my fortune?" he chuckled. "Please do! Make the future reveal that you will grant my greatest desire!"

She nodded amusedly, and rising, moved to a chest at one side of the tent. From it she took a large metal spoon, which she filled with lead shavings. This she held for several minutes over the lamp; and when the lead had become a molten mass, she poured it quickly into a cup of cold water. The abrupt change of temperature caused the molten metal to solidify and form in irregular pattern at the bottom of the cup. Zola then poured off the water, and presented Neal with the residue, as a token of her necromancy.

"Look at it closely, from all angles," she instructed. "Soon it will appear to be the outline of a human face. The face will be that of your worst enemy!"

"Wonderful!" he exclaimed, turning the object 'round and 'round. "You're a very clever girl, Zola!"

At first, he hoped the profile outlined in lead might prove to be that of his wife; he next wondered if it would bear resemblance to King Rom, Zola's father. But, in the end, he was obliged to conclude that his worst enemy must be a person as yet unknown.

"Why not," he asked seriously, "cast a picture of yourself, the girl who is destined to be mine?"

She cuddled close to him, linking her arm with his. "I do not predict delightful happenings," she explained. "I had rather cause them to come true!"

"Darling!" he whispered, slipping the lead souvenir into his pocket, and turning to claim her lips.

The lamp burned smokily upon the table, casting strange shadows on the walls of the tent. The silence of the night seemed to grow and deepen. And they had ears and eyes only for each other. She wrapped her arms about his neck. The loose front of her waist slipped slightly open, revealing much that it might have concealed.

Neal lowered his head and nestled in his lips in the smooth curving hollow of her throat. He heard her catch her breath as she felt his kiss.

"Zola!" he muttered huskily. "Little Gypsy darling!"

IT WAS WELL past midnight when Neal finally left the tent and stole silently back to his car—still later when he arrived home.

Yet, bright and early the following morning, he was back at the scene of the night's adventure—anxious, eager, for another glimpse of the dusky beauty who had so delighted him with her charms. The early morning sun was climbing swiftly over the treetops, as he parked beside the road and descended from the car.

But even at this early hour, the campsite was deserted! Tents, wagons, horses, dogs—all were gone! The Gypsies had risen before dawn, broken camp, and left on their never-ending pilgrimage. Not now would gypsy fiddles wail and sing in the clearing beside the road, or gypsy women dance about the flickering fire. Now remained but the cold, dead embers of that fire, like memories of a passion that has passed.

Neal reached into his pocket and drew out the tiny bit of lead—the irregular pattern that, Zola had said, bore the features of his worst enemy. For a long moment he stared at it, then thrust it back into his pocket.

"It resembles me!" he muttered. "I'm my own worst enemy! I've fallen in love with a girl I'll never see again! What could be worse than that?"

He turned disconsolately back toward his car. And the wailing tones of gypsy fiddles, heard in fancy, seemed to mock him. . . .

mured, pointedly, his gaze hovering for a moment upon a luscious bosom so attractively encased in velvet.

She made a mock curtsy. "Thank you, sir!" she whispered, smiling. "Just for that, I'll ride to the club in your car."

"Joyous news!" he grinned. "And let's be on our way. We want to get there before midnight, don't we?"

Mabel had linked arms with Don, and had left the dining room.

"Going to ride with me?" he asked, patting her hand.

"We were making ourselves pretty for you!" she said, fluttering her lashes at him.

"Why not?" she smiled.

They were seated in his car when Sylvia descended the bungalow steps with Paul.

"Tra-la-la!" Mabel waved to them as Don started.

"We'll be seeing you!" cried Sylvia.

DON GUIDED the roadster onto the main highway, and at a leisurely pace proceeded in the direction of the low lying foothills where the club was situated in a spot ideally suited to the rambling terrain of a golf course and the more hilarious devotees of dancing.

"You're prettier every time I see you!" he remarked, trying to keep one eye on Mabel and one on the road ahead. "How do you do it?"

"It's quite a strenuous life!" she laughed. "You've no idea how hard it is for us girls to live up to the compliments you men pay us . . . providing, of course, we believe you, which we don't."

Her wrap was suspended carelessly from her shoulder, and the small apples of her breasts were clearly limned under the satin of her gown. They looked just little enough to fit snugly into a manly palm, yet soft enough to thrill.

Don vowed that some day, or some night, he would ascertain just how perfectly those breasts would fit into his palm, and how sweet her red mouth would taste in a kiss. . . . Not that he hadn't attempted to do both of those delightful things. . . . But Mabel had always kept him at arm's length in a tantalizing way that seemed to mean: *"not-yet-but-soon . . . maybe!"*

In the art of flirtation, that was Mabel's technique. She liked to dangle herself before the eyes and senses of a man, and subconsciously thrill to the amative urge she aroused in him. She wanted to feel that men desired her, though she was not very desirous of men.

(*Please turn to page* 57)

FRENCH MODEL PHOTOS

MEN: Get a complete assortment of Real French Type Pictures, all different. Two sets (20) different Poses, Snappy Models in reclining and other poses. One set (12) different poses, young couples in passionate love scenes. Also a couple of Paris Models—the good stuff. All Clear, well made, gloss finished, quality pictures. These are all ACTUAL photographs.

Special: Some Short Stories, and over 50 small size pictures included with the above without extra charge, also a snappy illustrated booklet. All sent Prepaid on receipt of $1.00 cash, money order or stamps.

All for $1.00

REX SALES CO.

4166 PARK AVENUE, DEPT. P. S., NEW YORK CITY

BOOKS on CORPORAL PUNISHMENT

Remarkable stories of Whippings inflicted on both sexes, disclosing the strange grip the Rod has had on men and women since the beginning of Time.

* * *

Also many other curious and absorbing volumes on strange amatory customs and practices,—unabridged, privately printed and unusually illustrated.

* * *

ILLUSTRATED booklet, handsomely printed, describing these volumes in great detail, sent free in sealed envelope to responsible adults only. Send stamp. State age. Postcards ignored.

THE GARGOYLE PRESS
Dept. M.G 70 Fifth Ave., New York

New Stuff for Men

MAGGIE and JIGGS

Tillie & Mac, Dumb Dora, Boss and Bubbles, Peaches & Browning, A French Stenographer, A Bachelor's Dream, A Model's Life, Adam and Eve, Kip and Alice, Harold Teen and Lillums, Toots and Alice, Toots and Casper, The Gumps, Winnie Winkle, Gus and Gussie, Barney Google and Spark Plug, Boob McNut and Pearl, Tillie the Toiler, A Broker's Stenographer, Mabel with the Old Fiddler, The Unfaithful Wife, What the Janitor Saw In An Artist's Studio, A Strip Poker Card Game, A Sales-Lady and a Scotchman, The Iceman on the Lookout, The Butler and the Misses Taking Her Morning Exercise. Also 32 high-grade glossy photos of Naughty French Poses. French Men and Women in French Style Love Scenes, all different poses. Also Women alone, in all different poses. And 9 photos of Beautiful French Models with Beautiful Figures, in Daring Poses taken from Life. All the above will be sent you prepaid for only $1.00.

CARRANO SALES COMPANY
NEW HAVEN, CONN. Dept. MG-12-TP.

Spicy-Photos, Booklets

For Adults Only. Each Book differently Illustrated. Tillie & Mack; Maggie & Jiggs; Toots & Caspar; Harold Tenn; Winnie Winkel & Moon Mullins. Also entirely NUDE pictures unretouched, post card size, in appealing & daring positions. All 6 Books and 4 pictures for $1. or 6 Books & 15 pictures for $2.

AMOR NOVELTY CO., 96 Fifth Ave., Dept. R-2, N. Y. C.

A Thousand Thrills

FOR TWO DOLLARS

"LOVE IS EVERYWHERE"

by Jean Maxwell

Ten Complete Stories!
33,000 Words!
One Dollar, Postpaid!

"CHAMPAGNE," by Diana Page

Ten Complete Stories!
33,000 Words!
One Dollar, Postpaid!

We don't have to tell you anything about Jean Maxwell and Diana Page! Their books are torrid tomes for red-blooded people!

Do you like sophisticated love-making? Do you want fireworks in every paragraph? Do you relish intimate descriptions of hectic love scenes and snappy illustrations, too?

Here they are, boys and girls! Young folks with natures like volcanoes! Flaming youth having its fling! Thrills, thrills, thrills! We're telling you!

The first story in each book alone is worth the price, and there are TEN stories in each volume! Don't delay! Send your dollar bills today and give yourself a real treat!

GRACE PUBLISHING CO.
Post Office Box No. 2, Station "H"
New York, N. Y.

MEN HELP YOUR GLANDS WITHOUT USING POWERFUL INTERNAL STIMULANTS. When the glands weaken from worry, dissipation, etc.—use **GLANDVIGO** externally. A real gland stimulant. Strengthens weak, abused glands. Renews natural powers, strength & vigor with quick, lasting results. A trial box will quickly convince you. Sent sealed 25c.; large box $1.00—C.O.D. 15c extra.

Freer & Dean (Dept. P) 265 W. 34th St., New York City

(*Continued from page 54*)

Her thoughts were wont to dwell upon "possibilities" and "probabilities".

"I wonder how it would feel if I let him kiss me?" she would think, when it would be a very easy matter to prove it for herself.

Sometimes, in the shadowy darkness, she would lie in bed and let her mind wander idly as she cupped a miniature breast in her undulating hand and fondled it tenderly: "I'll bet he would love to do this!" she would murmur.

She wasn't thinking of Paul, asleep in the twin bed beside her. She might be referring to Tom, Dick or Harry, or any one of a dozen masculine acquaintances. "And that isn't all!" she'd sigh, clasping her pillow and closing her eyes, perchance to dream divinely!

Now, sitting by Don in his roadster, her agile imagination, spurred by cocktails and highballs, toyed with the possibilities inherent in his evdent attractiveness for her and attraction to her.

"You promised me a kiss!" he reminded her.

"When?" she smiled.

"Don't you remember?" he said, leaning toward her, but carefully gripping the wheel with both hands. "We were finished with the bridge game at your house, and I was watching you mix a cocktail in the pantry? You said: *'Not tonight . . . tomorrow'!*"

"Yes, I remember!" she laughed. "That's what I meant . . . not tonight, but tomorrow."

"Well, isn't this the time and place?"

"Oh, no! . . . This is tonight, not tomorrow."

Don heaved a sigh. "Then tomorrow never comes."

"You're wrong!" she whispered. "There's always a tomorrow!"

She could have planted a moist kiss on his lips then and there, even though he was driving carefully, and the very thought of it made her squirm.

"Sweet!" she thought. "It would be sweet!"

Don was speaking. "If there is anything I hate, it's tomorrow. . . . I'm a great believer in the motto: 'Do it now'!"

She smiled blissfully. She had drawn her wrap around her, and under it her hand was gently motivating the softness of a breast.

"Don't rush me, Don!" she whispered.

The car swerved into the grounds of the

country club, and there was a cynical smile on his lips.

IN THE MEANTIME, Sylvia and Paul had settled themselves in the car parked in front of the Harwood's bungalow. The street was a tree-lined thoroughfare, shadowy and dim.

She laid a hand on his arm. "I haven't had my kiss tonight!" she murmured.

"I didn't get a chance!" he replied, grinning. The lights on the dashboard hadn't yet been switched on.

"This is your chance!" she said, challengingly.

His arm went around her shoulder, and her shiny blonde head fell back on the seat. Under her cloak his hand wormed its way to travel over the smooth skin of bare arms and neck and press the soft abundance of voluptuous breasts.

"Mmmmm!" gasped Sylvia, twisting her mouth away. "All hot and bothered tonight, aren't you?"

"Why tonight, particularly?" he smiled.

"You never kissed me quite like that before!" she murmured.

"Give me another!" he pleaded.

"Oh, you bad man!" she cried. "I said my kiss . . . not kisses. . . . We usually have one kiss, don't we?"

"But isn't it time that we advanced from one kiss into several of them?" He was seeking her lips, but she swayed her face from side to side, evading him.

"Oh, you like a progressive game, don't you?" she said. "It does seem that we are progressing, fast and furiously."

She dropped her glance to his hand and suddenly placed her own hand on the fingers that were traveling slowly but steadily along a swelling thigh.

"Paul, darling, be yourself!" she sighed. But the fingers went on their way, even with her own accompanying hand, and it seemed to Paul as though she was really guiding instead of deterring his caress, while her face stopped swaying.

His lips clung to hers. Sylvia wound her arm about his neck.

For one blissful minute their faces were an indistinguishable blur in the shadows, then, with a sigh, Sylvia tore herself away.

"Phew!" she whistled. "Mama, mama, buy me that!"

Paul hugged her. "It isn't for sale, beautiful . . . it's given away free, gratis and for nothing to a girl like you."

Her arm vanished from his neck.

"*You Do Something To Me!*" she sang, softly, drawing his hand very determinedly away from her thigh, and sitting bolt upright so as to let his fingers drop from her breast.

"After that kiss, Paul, a cigarette is indicated!" she laughed, a throbbing, emotional note in its echo.

"I could sing that song, too!" he said, moodily.

"I wouldn't be at all surprised!" she murmured.

She had ridden in the front seat enough with Paul to know that there was a compartment in the dashboard always plentifully supplied with his cigarettes, and an electric lighter was there, also. . . . She bent toward it, and then she recalled Mabel's warning not to "stoop". . . . From the velvet decolletage of her gown her breasts surged forth rebelliously, and a ticklish thrill went through her as she realized that Paul's eyes must have seen much more than he had ever seen before.

Those breasts were still tingling from the contact of his fingers, and her lips were yet warm and moist from his kiss as she held the flame of the electric torch to the cigarette. . . . And hot young blood burned in her veins as flamingly as the torch itself.

Sylvia went much further in her flirtations than Mabel. . . . The latter liked to look at forbidden fruit and wonder how it would taste. . . . But the former liked to taste it without actually eating.

Sylvia's yearning for Paul was as keen as Mabel's longing for Don, physically, but Sylvia had gone no further than an occasional kiss and caress, while Mabel was still imagining things!

"Have a puff!" asked Sylvia, holding the cigarette to Paul's lips.

He inhaled deeply.

"It's lovely here, isn't it?" said Sylvia. "So quiet and peaceful!"

She slumped down in her seat, and a slippered toe tapped against the dashboard of the car. Her skirt slid backward along a silk stocking.

"What pretty knees!" murmured Paul.

She dropped the skirt. "There's a dimple three inches away from my garter!" she smiled. "It's even prettier than the knee."

"May I peek?"

"Oh, you naughty man!"

"Just one little peep!"

"Only one!"

She slowly pulled the skirt upward, past

her crossed knees until the edge of the gartered stocking appeared. . . . Further the skirt traveled, and Paul switched on the dashboard lights just in time to see a smooth bit of skin on a creamy thigh and a dimple that was alluringly plain. . . . Quickly the skirt fell like a curtain.

"There, you've had your peek!" said Sylvia, laughing.

"I'd like to kiss it!" he declared.

She put out a hand to switch off the lights. "That would be real progress, wouldn't it?" she murmured. "From that point goodness knows where you would go."

"I know!" he grinned.

"And I can imagine!" she smiled.

"Look at that vacant porch and the couch hammock!" He pointed to the bungalow. "It's a shame to have it go to waste on a night like this, isn't it? Besides, it would be much more comfortable than sitting in the front seat of an automobile."

She laughed. "Paul Creston! You're forgetting that we're on our way to a dance at the club."

"But a couch hammock with you is to be desired infinitely more than a crowded dance floor." He seized her hand, took another puff of the cigarette, and then kissed her palm.

"You are a big, bold, bad man!" she smiled. "What would my husband think if we were conspicuous by our absence at that dance? Not to mention what your wife might think!"

"We could show up later!" he said, lamely.

"It'll be later, anyway!" She consulted her wrist-watch. "We've been sitting here for fifteen minutes already."

His arm lay along the back of the seat. Thumb and forefinger pulled her cloak from a bare shoulder. "Your skin is just like satin!" he said.

"Thanks, darling, but we ought to be getting along to the club." She flipped the cigarette through the open window, and watched it fall in a shower of sparks on the road.

"Let's run in and have another highball!" he suggested.

"How scandalous!" she murmured.

"Or you can mix a couple of those famous cocktails of yours!" he continued.

"Really?"

"Why not?"

His fingertips were traversing the warmth of her bare back, and it was an easy matter for his hand to slide under the velvet below her arm and make contact with a pulsing breast.

"Paul!" she remonstrated, but not very severely. "You seem to be confident that this is going to be the night of all nights!"

"Isn't it?" he muttered, pressing his lips to her shoulder.

"What makes you think so?" she laughed. "Because we kissed that way just now, and because I'm permitting . . . this?"

She laid her hand over the fingers that were embedded in the jellied softness of a mound. "Convenient gown, isn't it?" she added.

"You're gorgeous!" he breathed, bending over her.

Backward she reclined, cuddling down in the seat. His lips were crushing her mouth fiercely, as she thought of the couch hammock, only a few short steps away!

(To be continued)

(Continued from page 7)

"Sure," her brother responded good naturedly; "he isn't a bad egg. Let's himself go pretty wide sometimes and we have to raid him to make him keep more under cover, else there'd be complaints to this office."

"Is he dangerous; that is, if you raided him would you be likely to get hurt?"

"No, Tony knows better than that; the mobs never shoot at men from this office."

"Then you'll do something just to please me?"

"You know damn well I'd do anything just to please you."

"Raid him, tonight."

"What for?"

"Just to please me."

"Well, I don't see how you're going to get any kick out of that; but, O. K. if you say so, I'll stop on my way home and put on a quiet little raid.

Lily sent him a kiss over the 'phone and hung up, to go back to her dreaming.

(Continued from page 2)

Dear Editor:

I've read every issue of Spicy for two years, so you know I like it or I wouldn't buy it. The stories are great, and your authors sure know their stuff; especially Jean Maxwell and Diana Page. But here's one criticism I'd like to give—couldn't you have fewer stories about such people as artists and writers, etc., and more about ordinary trades and professions? I think a lot of your readers would enjoy them more. But maybe I'm wrong—how about hearing from somebody else on the subject?

Outside of that I think Spicy is the best magazine on the stands, and I never miss a copy!

Sincerely yours,
Larry Greely.

Detroit, Mich.

Dear Editor:

Good for you! The September issue of Spicy Stories is a wow! I've written before to tell you how much I like your magazine—maybe repetition will make you believe I mean it.

My favorite authors are Tom Kane, Gordon Sayre, and Kay Carroll, but all of them are good. What I wanted especially to mention is the cover picture. I wonder if the other readers appreciate the dandy covers you've been having on Spicy as much as I do. This picture of the girl with the cocktail is a knockout! Give us more like that.

Yours sincerely,
Jack Millerton.

Shreveport, La.

(Continued from page 38)

ing neckline of her dress. Kirk let it slip, but the hand that guided it paused on damp hillocks, quivering to his touch.

"Thank the rain," he murmured.

"Kirk!" she breathed passionately. "Give me love!"

"Love and everything that goes with it," he whispered, slipping the wet dress from her shoulders. "That disease I told you about—*magnorum feminarum*—comes from too many women, but it's easily cured by one woman who can be herself and not somebody else. Will you be the doctor?"

Kitty thrilled to the touch of his fingers on her skin. She swayed against him. "Yes," she panted, "and I prescribe love?"

"In big doses!" he agreed.

A flash of lightning seemed to fuse them as one.

KITTY'S WIRE to Bobby was short and explicit:

Need a secretary and chauffeur Stop
Yes Question Mark
Mrs. Kirk Duncan.

Bobby's wire was shorter, more explicit:

Yes Exclamation Point
Mrs. Mike Dougherty.

(Continued from page 29)

"Roger," she cried, tears of joy coursing down her cheeks.

Gently he lifted her, carrying her inert form to the bed.

"Darling," she whispered, between kisses, "after our 'honeymoon', suppose we make this 'our room' instead of 'mine'?"

"Idiot!" he grinned, "why do you suppose you're getting a honeymoon?"

(Continued from page 46)

murmured, joyously, a hand cupping the yielding firmness of a breast. "We're young only once, aren't we? . . . And . . . after we're married . . ."

A weak sigh echoed in the hallway. "It isn't so *very* late, after all, is it?" she whispered. "You can come in . . . for a little while!"

Half a Million People

have learned music this easy way

YES, over half a million delighted men and women all over the world have learned music this quick easy way.

Half a million—what a gigantic orchestra they would make! Some are playing on the stage, others in orchestras, and many thousands are daily enjoying the pleasure and popularity of being able to play some instrument.

Surely this is convincing proof of the success of the **new modern method** perfected by the U.S. School of Music! And what these people have done, YOU, too, can do!

Many of this half million didn't know one note from another—others had never touched an instrument—yet in half the usual time, they learned to play their favorite instrument. Best of all, they found learning music **amazingly** easy. No monotonous hours of exercises—no tedious scales—no expensive teachers. This simplified method made learning music as easy as A-B-C!

It is like a fascinating game. From the very start you are playing **real** tunes, perfectly by **notes.** You simply can't go wrong, for every step, from beginning to end, is right before your eyes in print and picture. First you are **told** how to do a thing, then a picture **shows** you how, then you do it yourself and **hear** it. And almost before you know it, you are playing your favorite pieces—jazz, ballads, classics. No private teacher could make it clearer. Little theory—plenty of accomplishment. That's why students of the U. S. School of Music get ahead twice as fast—**three times as fast** as those who study old-fashioned, plodding methods.

You don't need any special "talent." Many of the half-million who have already become accomplished players never dreamed they possessed musical ability. They only wanted to play some instrument—just like you—and they found they could quickly learn how this easy way. Just a little of your spare time each day is needed—and you enjoy every minute of it. The cost is surprisingly low—averaging only a few cents a day—and the price is the same for whatever instrument you choose. And remember, you are studying right in your own home—without paying big fees to private teachers.

Don't miss any more good times! Learn now to play your favorite instrument and surprise all your friends. Change from a wallflower to the center of attraction. Music is the best thing to offer at a party—musicians are invited everywhere. Enjoy the popularity you have been missing. Get your share of the musician's pleasures and profit! Start now!

What Instrument for You?

Piano
Organ
Violin
Clarinet
Flute
Harp
Cornet
'Cello
Guitar
Ukulele
Saxophone
Piccolo
Hawaiian Steel Guitar
Drums And Traps
Mandolin
Sight Singing
Trombone
Piano Accordion
Banjo (Plectrum, 5-String or Tenor)
Voice and Speech Culture
Harmony and Composition
Automatic Finger Control
Italian and German Accordion
Junior's Piano Course
Trumpet

Free Booklet and Demonstration Lesson

If you are in earnest about wanting to join the crowd of entertainers and be a "big hit" at any party—if you really **do** want to play your favorite instrument, to become a performer whose services will be in demand—fill out and mail the convenient coupon asking for our Free Booklet and Free Demonstration Lesson. These explain our wonderful method fully and show you how easily and quickly you can learn to play at little expense. This booklet will also tell you all about the amazing new **Automatic Finger Control.** U. S. School of Music, 45811 Brunswick Bldg., New York City.

NRA MEMBER U.S.
WE DO OUR PART

Thirty-sixth Year (Established 1898)

U. S. SCHOOL OF MUSIC,
45811 Brunswick Bldg., New York City

Please send me your free book, "How You Can Master Music in Your Own Home," with inspiring message by Dr. Frank Crane, Free Demonstration Lesson and particulars of your easy payment plans. I am interested in the following course:

. . . . Have you instrument? . . . .

Name . . . .

Address . . . .

City . . . . State . . . .

www.ingramcontent.com/pod-product-compliance
Lightning Source LLC
LaVergne TN
LVHW061254100826
845148LV00008B/1124